Hello

THE MASKS OF
ROBIN HOOD

Louise Dale

Dragonheart
Publishing

Published in Great Britain in 2007 by
Dragonheart Publishing,
PO BOX 948
Lincoln
LN5 5EH

www.dragonheartpublishing.co.uk

British Cataloguing in Publication Data.
A catalogue record of this book is available from the British
Library

ISBN 978-0-9543773-5-9

Cover painting by Ian R. Ward, Mansfield, Nottinghamshire

The Time Trigger Series:
The Masks of Robin Hood
Royal Pirates
Savage Pilgrims
Millennium Spies
The Keys of Rome
The Curse of Rocamadour

Typesetting and production by
Richard Joseph Publishers Ltd, PO Box 15, Devon EX38 8ZJ

Printed in Great Britain by Creative Print & Design, Wales.

Lythe and listin, gentilmen,
That be of frebore blode.
I shall you tel of a gode yeman,
His name was Robyn Hode.

From: **A Gest of Robyn Hode**
First fytte (part one)
Compiled and printed in the fifteenth century,
Possibly as early as 1400 A.D.

(Give ear and listen, gentlemen,
Who are of freeborn blood.
I shall tell you of a good yeoman,
His name was Robin hood.)

Author's Note

Was Robin Hood real? This was an exam question for my daughter's GCSE in history. Like a classic book, this legend is so cemented into contemporary life as to find itself the subject of discussion in examinations. According to historical scholars, there have been so many possible contenders for Robin Hood from yeomen and servants to knights, all having been recorded living across Yorkshire and Nottinghamshire in the area once known as Sherwood Forest over several centuries. Nothing was written down in the early medieval period and the legend has been passed down by word of mouth like a Chinese whisper and written down in poems like the famous *A Gest of Robyn Hode* of the fifteenth century. The story has been heavily embellished, its philosophies and characters distorted over the centuries. We shall never know the answer to the question "was Robin Hood real?" But it does not matter. Like all good stories, its purpose is to entertain and that it will surely continue to do, evolving further to suit the cultures and politics of the next millennium.

I have used this multi-faceted evidence and the many theories to create my own fictional theory: that Robin Hood was a hoax created to hide the identities of the guardians of some of the most powerful Time Triggers ever known, in my fictional world of those who have the power to surf the waves of time in the battle between good and evil.

The text generally accepted as being the earliest

evidence is the *Gest*, and from that I have drawn much information. I am also much indebted to J.C. Holt's excellent *Robin Hood* (1988) and to Tony Molyneux-Smith's *Robin Hood and the Lords of Wellow* (1998) for their theories, as well as countless other writers across the world whose work I have read on the internet and in the library.

I have lived in Sherwood Forest for many years so I draw much from my own local knowledge and also thank the work of Nottinghamshire County Council at their various tourist attractions and visitor centres.

As always, this is a work of fiction and the characters are pure fantasy. It is designed to provide hours of fun reading and to encourage a love of books. However there is much blending with researched history in the hope that some young readers may be stimulated to go on to research this and other fascinating stories that make the subject of history one of the most relevant and vital in our modern age.

Louise Dale
2007

Contents

For Lizzie, Em, Rich, Mum and Dad

*Thank you too, to Richard Joseph,
for great friendship and advice.*

1

Greenwood

The arrow hissed past Robert's ear splicing the bark behind him with a powerful thud. Alice gasped. They were surrounded. There was nowhere to run.

The circle of archers parted for a single horse. Their leader leapt from his animal. Rays of sunlight pierced the forest canopy above and reflected from the man's sword to dance across his cruel face. Alice's grip on Robert's hand tightened.

"Keep still. We'll be O.K.," said Robert. "Someone needs us very much alive to have gone to the trouble of getting us here. They needed us enough to have arranged for us to get this Time Trigger."

He looked down at the jewel in his other hand. Robert knew it must be one of the rare objects connected with the past called Time Triggers. Its forces had awoken their own special time travelling powers once again. This one had mysteriously found its way into Robert's pencil case at school and instead of Robert or Alice deciding where and when they would travel to with it, someone else's thoughts had directed them to here. Robert's heart raced as he wondered why. At last they were starting out on a quest again.

He slid the Time Trigger jewel next to his mobile phone in the safety of the inside pocket of his blazer.

The tall leader began to walk towards them. Robert felt a fleeting flicker of recognition somewhere deep in his memories. Then, to Robert's surprise, the man slid his sword into its sheath and offered him his hand to shake. He was a heavily built man with silver grey hair. He wore a red velvet cloak trimmed with gold over his armour.

"Looks like a knight or something," said Alice under her breath.

"Dear boy, I was wondering how long it would take for you to reach us," boomed the man.

He smiled widely, showing a lot of white teeth. Robert knew that hygiene in the Middle Ages was not great and he couldn't help thinking that these impressive molars were unusually white, even for a knight. The man turned to Alice.

"You are truly as lovely as the minstrels' tales foretold, my Lady. Welcome to the world at the end of the thirteenth century and to our battle," he said.

"I'm sorry, I don't understand," said Alice. "I think you may have mixed us up with someone?"

"Nonsense, dear girl. No need to be modest." The man's voice was deep and powerful. "Now don't be shy. The ballads tell of your bravery and courage. You are both famous. I can only say how pleased I am that you have chosen wisely and have come straight to me. Welcome young Master Robert. Or should I say Master Hood?"

"My surname is Davenport," said Robert. "Not, er...Hood."

"As you wish," said the man, smirking unpleasantly. He glanced behind, wary of the approach of another.

"Sheriff, we must pull back," said a boy. "The castle archers will soon reach us with their arrows. Your squire thinks we should return to Nottingham and collect more men."

"The Sheriff of... Nottingham?" said Robert, almost whispering.

The man stared at Robert. He bowed. His creepy smile had vanished.

"Well, well. You know me, but can it be that you two do not yet know your own destinies? Do you not know what it is that you must do?" he said. "Well, there is no time to enlighten you now if I am to lay siege to Sir Richard's castle. This part of the business is up to me. Your time is after."

Robert looked at Alice. She shrugged back, looking equally confused.

"Stay here at my encampment on this side of the Greenwood," said the Sheriff. "My page will escort you. You will be taken care of, trust me. When I have vanquished the traitor I will return and we can talk some more about your...ancestry. Why don't you practice your archery skills and we will have a tournament when I am done?"

He strode towards his horse and galloped off, leading his men in a cloud of dust, leaving a strange quietness in the forest.

Robert looked at the Sheriff's page. Underneath his cowled hood the boy looked about twelve years old, like himself. He had a mop of flaxen blond hair like Robert. But unlike Robert, whose eyes were bright blue, this boy had brown eyes. They were large and round and shone like stones in a clear stream.

"What's your name?" said Alice.

"Thomas of Wellow, my Lady," said the boy, smiling.

"My Lady who....?"

"Lady Marion," interrupted Robert. "This young man will no doubt take us to where we can rest." Robert winked at Alice. She looked as if she was about to protest. "Is that not so, Thomas?"

"Yes, Master...Hood," said the boy. He grinned at Robert. "This way. It is just in the clearing there."

Alice grimaced at Robert.

11

"Play along with him," hissed Robert. ". . . until we know what's going on."

The young page led them down a rough track through the trees. Robert and Alice lived in Newark in Nottinghamshire and had been to Sherwood Forest lots of times. Robert had seen the Major Oak and jousting festivals, but this undergrowth was much denser than the modern forest he knew. The trees were so close a squirrel could jump from tree to tree for miles in a straight line. There were no modern roads or buildings anywhere in sight and certainly no visitor centre brimming with tourists. The rough foliage scratched Alice's bare legs above her navy blue school socks.

Very soon they emerged into a small clearing. In front of them were numerous shacks built with branches against the smaller tree trunks and covered with animal skins or brushwood. The enormous leafy spread of one mighty oak protected the entire encampment like a giant umbrella over a football pitch.

There was no one about. Smoke curled into the canopy of leaves from a fire in front of the largest of the dwellings. Someone was shouting inside.

Thomas waved them in, laughing.

"Don't worry about the fat monk," he said. "He is the Sheriff's cook. At least that's what he tries to do here. The Sheriff's men only made camp yesterday. The women may join us if the siege looks like being a long one. The Sheriff thinks the friar will guard you, but I promise he is a friend."

Robert was just about to ask more when sounds of clattering metal erupted through the doorway of the big shack. Alice and Robert followed Thomas inside. For a make-shift dwelling, it had some large pieces of furniture and tapestries.

"Someone is rich enough to have all the comforts of home brought along to battle," said Alice.

A meaty smell mingled with something strong and fruity. As his eyes adjusted to the dim light, Robert saw a rotund figure dressed in brown sackcloth robes held closed with a rope belt. His hair was shaved on the top of his head and an enormous floppy hood hung across the man's shoulders. He stirred a cauldron of broth suspended over the fire with one hand and slurped drink from a flagon in the other. He burped, wiped his mouth with the back of his greasy hand and smiled at the visitors.

"Well Thomas, who have we here?" he said. His grin revealed his many missing teeth.

"These are the two our true master has been speaking of. The ones who will help him. The Lady Marion and...."

"Robin Hood?" said the monk, letting go of his oversized ladle. Robert watched it sink out of sight into the meaty froth. "Holy Mary! Is it you again?"

2

The Secret Sign

The monk stood up. He looked about them suspiciously before closing the door and shooting the heavy bolt across. The room had a strange herbal smell that was strongest close to the monk where medicinal herbs had rubbed off on his robes.

"Sit," he said.

His face was serious now and he was sweating even more. He pushed Alice towards an oak table.

Robert saw the fear in his eyes.

"Give me the sign, so that I can be sure you are who you claim to be," said the monk when they were all seated on the bench seats.

Robert and Alice looked at one another in confusion.

"The sign!" shouted the monk. He produced a dagger from his robes and began to stand up. "If you do not show it, I will be forced to kill you."

Thomas leapt up.

"Friar, surely there is no need for such aggression?" he said.

"Silence, boy!" said the monk. "You know nothing."

"Just a minute," said Alice. She looked at Robert and pointed towards the inside of his blazer.

Suddenly he knew what she was trying to say. He slowly reached into the pocket and withdrew the Time Trigger. It glowed red in the firelight as he held it up between his finger and thumb. He heard the monk gasp. If they closed their eyes and concentrated their power, they would travel backwards or forwards on the spot. If they really focused, they would control the forces locked in this Trigger and create a Time Tunnel, a translucent structure, almost invisible to normal people, that would allow them to travel safely to a different location as well. Someone had created one for them to get here in the first place and for a fleeting second, Robert wondered if he had yet met that someone, or were there other players in this mission?

There wasn't time to worry about that yet. The monk was staring at the Time Trigger. Robert focused his mind. With his other hand he grasped Alice's wrist under the table. He closed his eyes. Drawing all the power from deep inside his body as quickly as he could, Robert willed himself to time travel, thinking hard of the school playground from where they had started only a short while before.

As the dazzling tube of energy enveloped them both, Robert heard the monk and Thomas shouting wildly. But before he could understand what they were saying, he opened his eyes amid the sunlight and chaos of the school lunch time. Their voices were drowned out by shrieks and laughter all around.

"Phew!" said Alice, pulling her wrist free from his tight grip. "So what sign is he on about then? If we don't figure this out quickly and those guys come after us, which is distinctly possible I should say, we could find ourselves stabbed or shot in the chest by an arrow pretty soon."

"And how come the ordinary people could see us?" said Robert. "Before, we've only been visible to other time travellers."

"Um, no idea," said Alice. "There are some dark influences lurking this time, Rob."

The bell rang for the start of afternoon school.

"What lesson have you got now?" said Alice.

"It's Friday, so it's double science with Mr Reynolds," said Robert.

"I've got French with the bossy new teacher, Miss Gilbert," groaned Alice. "Shall we meet after school by the gates?"

Robert nodded and plodded off to join the swarm of children flocking inside. As he tried to manoeuvre through the double entrance doors, he felt a sharp pull on his shoulder. He reeled backwards expecting to see a gruesome face threatening him. Instead some older boys sniggered. His back pack had snagged on the door hinges as he was jostled by them.

"What's the matter, Davenport? You look like you've seen a deadly ghost!" said one.

For a moment they surrounded him menacingly.

"We should kill you, burn your school bag and take your pretty girlfriend!" hissed their dark haired leader.

Robert stood still, hoping to seem boring if he did not retaliate. They sniggered at one another before sloping off down the now deserted corridor.

"Bandits! You should get a job with the Sheriff of Nottingham," muttered Robert to himself.

With a shudder and a little look over his shoulder, Robert opened the door of the science room.

"Ah, Robert Davenport," said Mr Reynolds. "I was worried about you. Where have you been?"

"Sorry, Sir," said Robert. "Had a bit of bother from some enemies earlier but I sorted it."

"Enemies?" said the tall teacher. He frowned. "What kind of enemy lurks in this school then?"

"Oh, dodgy sheriffs and violent monks," said Robert flippantly.

Mr Reynolds stiffened. He stood up even taller. He

was a heavily built but athletic man with a black beard and moustache. He also taught fencing and karate as well as being the head of science. Some boys had nicknamed him 'Little Science' as a kind of joke because he was actually so big. Now he was looking at Robert strangely. Robert regretted his silly remark. He didn't want to get detention after school. Not tonight. The whole class had gone quiet, sensing the possibility of a spectacle.

"I'm sorry, Sir. I don't know what I meant by that," said Robert.

"Were you hurt?" said Mr Reynolds.

Robert was surprised. That was not the response he was expecting. Mr Reynolds wasn't usually dramatic or sarcastic.

"Um, no," said Robert.

Mr Reynolds glanced at the watching class. He coughed and turned back to them.

"Take your seat, Davenport," he said without looking at Robert. "And see me after school in my office."

Robert flinched. That was going to make him late for meeting Alice.

He tried to concentrate on the lesson. Somehow the structure of electric circuits didn't seem as interesting as usual. Robert even struggled to concentrate on his favourite practical part, fitting extra batteries into the circuit to make the little light bulb shine brighter.

He kept worrying about the sign the monk had asked for. What sign? Was it an actual thing or possibly some sort of code? Was it something he had been given and not noticed?

"Robert! That's enough batteries!" said a boy. "You'll make the bulbs explode!"

He looked down at what he was doing.

"I doubt that's possible," said Robert.

Then he saw it. The little bulbs were shinning really brightly in a circle. It reminded him of the scorched circles left by Time Tunnels.

He had doodled this shape on his pencil cases and school books ever since the first time he had seen the smouldering mark when they had met the dangerous King Canute on another quest. It was a circle with lines shooting out to represent the light and forces of a Time Tunnel. He'd even etched a tiny one with his compass inside one of the old style desks in the history room and scratched lots of little lines around it.

"The sign," he murmured.

Robert's time travelling powers were growing all the time. So were Alice's. They had changed from novices to Time Regents now. Each time they found a Time Trigger their powers magnified. They had been able to rescue a hostage from a Time Cage and had already defeated some dangerous Regents who had turned their powers to evil.

Robert knew this was the start of their next quest. But this one felt bad already. He shivered. Somehow he felt he was going to face his worst challenge yet.

But at least he had a probable solution for the sign the monk had asked for, in case he found himself back in the medieval forest again. He drew the sign on the palm of his left hand with a biro.

He felt inside his blazer pocket. Someone had deliberately left the shiny little gemstone in his pencil case. But who? And why? Who were his friends and who really were his enemies?

He felt another pull on his shoulder. This time it was somebody's hand.

3

Blood Stain

"Whatever it is that you are dreaming about Robert, I hope it will help you with your revision paper tonight," said Mr Reynolds.

"Er, yes Sir. It will," said Robert. He remembered the end of term exams with slight anxiety.

"And please take some of those batteries out of your circuit," said Mr Reynolds. "Do you want to send us all back in time with your power or something?"

Robert stared at Mr Reynolds in horror. The teacher was smiling mischievously. Robert studied him. Did this man know about him? Was he a time traveller too? Mr Reynolds had taken up his job as head of science at the beginning of this school year, at the same time Robert and Alice moved up from primary school. Robert had never really taken much notice of him. He was one of the better teachers though, who always made lessons interesting and who never got steamed up about little things. He was a really good fencing coach too.

The bell rang.

"Tidy up the lab please," shouted Mr Reynolds. "And hand in your revision paper next Monday. That gives you two whole days to do it."

"Great! Thanks Little Science! No life this weekend then," murmured one of the boys. "Got time for a film tomorrow though, Rob?"

"Maybe," said Robert. "I'll text you."

"Oh. Very mysterious," said the boy. "Meeting Alice are you?"

Robert frowned at him.

"We're just friends," he said, trying not to sound cross.

"Whatever," said the other boy. "Look out. Here comes the big man to remind you about your little visit to his office."

"I know, Sir," said Robert. "I'm coming."

"Were you alone when you had your little spot of bother earlier or was young Alice Hemstock with you by any chance?" said Mr Reynolds. Robert had to stop himself staring with his mouth open. "Because if she was there, she'd better come to my office with you. I'll meet you both in my room in ten minutes."

Mr Reynolds turned and left the room.

Robert flipped out his mobile phone and started texting Alice urgently. The classroom door flew open before he could finish.

He looked up.

"Caught you!" shouted Alice.

"It's you I'm texting!" said Robert. He was breathing fast. "I'm pretty sure I know what the sign is. Oh and I think we might have a problem with Mr Reynolds."

"That's funny," said Alice. "I had a problem with the warty Miss Gilbert. She was really nasty to me. She kept criticising my accent and gave me extra homework. There was one moment when she caught me doodling ideas about who might be behind this quest. I thought I could feel a shadow behind me. I don't know how long she'd been looking over my shoulder."

"Well Mr Reynolds is well dodgy," said Robert. "If he doesn't know something about all this, he must be telepathic. He's got to be a time traveller. The question is whether he's on our side or against us.

He wants to see us in his office. I'm not sure we should get too close on our own with him. He's too big for even both of us to tackle."

"I think we'd better go though," said Alice thoughtfully. "I've got a feeling that's what we're meant to do. Somebody's got to give us some more information. Maybe we will be walking into the lion's den, so to speak, but I don't know what choice we've got."

"You're right. I trust your hunches and feelings. It must be a girlie-intuition-thing I don't have, I suppose," said Robert grinning.

Alice slapped him affectionately across his head.

"So what are your thoughts about this sign thing?" she said.

Robert pulled out his planner and pointed to the doodles he had made all over the cover.

"That thing you're always scribbling everywhere?" said Alice. "But...maybe! Rob, you know, I think you could be right! You told me not so long ago how you couldn't get that shape out of your mind. Maybe it's been lurking in your subconscious waiting to be used."

"Pity we don't know what the sign will do for us though," said Robert.

"Stay close," said Alice, opening the door and peering out. "If we get into trouble, grip the Trigger gem stone and get us out to somewhere else."

"Any requests?" said Robert shoving his bag on one shoulder as they walked down the deserted corridor.

Everyone else had gone home now and it was eerily quiet.

"I'd like to say a beach in Florida or something, but I'm sure your mind will fix on somewhere more practical," said Alice.

Robert knocked on the door of Mr Reynolds' office. There was no reply. He knocked again and the door creaked ajar. He looked at Alice.

"Odd," he said quietly.

He pushed the door open with his fingertips.

There was no-one inside.

"Look!" said Alice.

Robert followed her gaze.

On the edge of the teacher's desk a pool of fresh red blood dripped slowly down the table leg and collected in a dark stain on the carpet below.

4

Rob-in-th'whode

Robert walked slowly round to the other side of the desk. Everything looked normal. Homework books were stacked in piles ready to be marked, towering above the jumble of pens, papers and dirty coffee cups. The computer was switched off.

"Hey, look at this," said Alice.

She was staring at a map of the world pinned to the wall. It was marked with lots of crosses with dates next to them, mostly in Great Britain, but some in other parts of Europe and some in Asia and North Africa and the Middle East.

"Look at these dates," she said. "They're all a long time ago. Eleven hundreds here. Thirteen and fourteen hundreds there. I wonder what it all means?"

Robert noticed a drawer in the desk that was slightly ajar. He bent down to look closer.

"I think there's more blood here. Somebody was either trying to open or close it," he said.

He picked up a ruler and prised the drawer open. He whistled.

"Look at these scrolls," he said.

He lifted out the top one. Gently, he released the leather ribbon and the parchment sprang open. The inside was covered with strange markings and letters that formed words in a foreign language. Alice gasped over Robert's shoulder. There in the centre was the symbol he had drawn so often; the circle of fire and light.

"Sshh!" whispered Alice.

There was a shuffling sound outside the door.

Robert shoved the scroll inside his blazer and pushed the drawer shut with his knee. As he did so, the computer screen sprang to life from its hibernation.

Someone slowly pushed open the door.

Robert didn't know which way to look. As the skinny, suited silhouette of Miss Gilbert, the French teacher, slithered into the room, he was distracted by the three words that flashed up in a large font on the screen.

ROBERT
ALICE
DANCE

Instinctively, he pressed the button to switch off the screen.

"And what, may I ask, are you two doing here?" said the teacher.

Her eyes were narrow and hostile, like snake's eyes in her bony face. Alice moved in front of the desk and stood in front of the dripping blood.

"Mr Reynolds asked us to meet him here," said Robert.

"He is not present though, is he? And you appear to be touching his desk," said Miss Gilbert.

"Er, no... and no," said Robert.

"Are you trying to be smart, Robert Davenport? Because if you are, you have picked the wrong person. Come out from behind that desk."

Robert deftly hopped around the side and stood next to Alice. The teacher inched towards them.

Robert started to feel sick.

The teacher was looking at him strangely. The power of her deep set eyes bore into him. The room started to spin round and round. He smelt something unpleasant. He shook his head and pressed

24

his hands on his ears.

Someone touched his blazer and then everything went black.

When he opened his eyes, Alice was shaking him.

"Get up, Rob!" she whispered. "We've time travelled. I picked your pocket and used the Time Trigger to get us out of there. Miss Gilbert was trying to hypnotise you or something. I'll swear she's not on our side."

Robert could hear the noise of men shouting and swords clashing just the other side of a thick area of forest undergrowth. He rolled onto his knees next to Alice.

"Over here," she said, pointing to an enormous tree trunk wide enough for a horse to hide behind. They crouched down and peered out.

"Those two men look like Norman soldiers," said Robert. "They are wearing some bits of armour. Their dark hair is shaved off round the back, like Normans on that Bayeaux Tapestry we saw pictures of in school. They're both fighting just one man, two against one. He looks different though. More like a peasant. He's only got an ordinary tunic on."

"He looks Saxon with that long blonde hair and garters," said Alice.

"He hasn't got a chance against those two," said Robert.

There was a squelching sound and the Saxon gave an agonising scream, clutching his stomach. Robert recoiled in horror. He felt sick and dizzy. Alice put her hands over her own mouth. Then a woman started to shout, struggling with the two men.

Robert looked at Alice.

"I think we should do something," he whispered.

"But we don't have any weapons," said Alice.

At that moment they heard the sound of horses'

hooves and more shouts. They ducked down. Robert peered carefully out. The two Normans trotted past on horses carrying blood-stained shields. Behind them, tied to the second horse's tail, was the woman. She ran, barefoot, trying to keep up with the horses. Behind the undergrowth, flames licked up into the air as her home burnt furiously.

"We have to do something," said Robert.

He started to stand up. Just as he was about to shout out, he felt a large hand across his mouth, gagging him.

"Silence, friend," came a deep voice. "I know who you are. I have been expecting you. Leave them to us."

Robert turned and the man gently released his hand. Another man held Alice. The first man signalled to Robert and Alice to be silent before slowly taking his hands away. More and more men melted out of the foliage around them and slid from behind tree trunks. They mostly wore tunics of a reddish brown colour over their woollen leg coverings and had small branches fastened to their hoods and even to their flat, medieval coif caps. Robert realised the foliage kept them camouflaged. Some even carried leaves in their mouths to perfect the disguise. None of them paid Alice and Robert any attention. They were moving silently at great speed through the forest, towards the two horsemen and their captive. The leader signalled for Robert and Alice to be very still. One by one, his men slid arrows from their backs and into their bows.

Suddenly the leader gave a battle cry and they launched their attack. Robert looked at Alice. She was grimacing in disgust as the thud of several arrows found their mark through the trees.

Robert knew the two horsemen were dead.

The leader returned. He was smiling. Behind him, Robert watched one of his men wrap a blanket around the sobbing woman.

"The Sheriff's mercenaries," said the leader. "Violent Norman bullies that prey on defenceless peasants. Pity we did not get word in time to save the husband. The woman will be well cared for back in the safety of our village though."

"Who are you?" said Alice.

The handsome young man propped his bow against a tree, pushed back his hood and grinned.

"The sign?" he said.

This time Robert drew the circle with lines coming out like flames in the dirt of the forest floor with his foot.

"Excellent. My name is Elias Foliot, knight of the realm and twelfth century Time Regent," said the man.

"We're in a different century from before," whispered Robert.

Alice nodded.

"I bid you come feast with me at my castle," said Sir Elias. "What you have just seen from my men is an example of the work of Rob-in-th'whode."

"Who's he?" said Alice.

"He is a *robber in the wood*," said Sir Elias. "He apparently robs the rich travellers and helps the poor forest folk."

The man and his men laughed loudly.

"We only protect our people. The ballad serves us well as a decoy, eh lads?" said Sir Elias. "When asked who did the deed, we can say t'was the work of Rob-in-th'whode. But I think you two youngsters will know this phrase as how it will come to be pronounced more famously."

"Robin Hood," murmured Alice.

5

Bows and Feathers

"For several generations, my people have found it useful to blame one 'Robin Hood' for happenings hereabouts. Especially to the Sheriff of Nottingham," said Sir Elias Foliot. "We are not outlaws but we do not answer to the fool's justice of anyone who claims authority, save the King himself. He is our sovereign. But there are many who hold high office as his sheriffs and as bishops and abbots who abuse their power over the people. For them I hold no respect and I will defend my people against their injustices."

Sir Elias led them through the trees on a rough track.

"You seem surprised at all this," said Sir Elias. "Surely you have been prepared by your guardian?"

"What do you mean?" said Alice, giving Robert a puzzled look.

Sir Elias Foliot stopped still.

"Do you mean to say you really do not understand why you are here?" he said.

Robert and Alice shook their heads.

"John has not spoken to you yet? You do not know about the masks?" Sir Elias Foliot whistled in surprise. "In that case it must fall to me to enlighten you before it is too late" He stared into the distance deep in thought. "Someone has tried to bring you here too soon. They are trying to outwit us. And I think I can guess which unpleasant character that must be. . . ."

"The Sheriff of Nottingham, I bet," said Robert,

the thrill of the new quest rising inside him..

"Exactly, my young friend," said the knight. "You speak as if you have met him."

"We have," said Alice.

"He is a Time Regent who has hidden behind the powerful office of the Sheriff of Nottingham in order to get close to the masks," said Sir Elias. Robert wanted to ask about these masks, but the knight continued. "He has chosen within himself to live on indefinitely without ageing, as any Time Regent may choose to do for a difficult quest. Little John has done the same. But this Sheriff is an evil Regent. I suspect when you encountered him, it was in another century. In my future?"

Alice and Robert nodded.

"It will have been in a time when it falls to my descendents to help John guard the masks," said Sir Elias. "I know all this because I have seen it in a Shell of Destiny."

"Oh, we've seen one of those shells before, and the window of visions that they can form," said Alice, grinning. "Do you have one?"

"It is not mine exactly," said Sir Elias. "I have used it as will my heirs but it really belongs to a great friend. Someone who I thought would be here now. The man who has taken on the duty of being the chief guardian and also your protector until the time was right. That man is Little John."

Sir Elias' brow furrowed in concern. He looked around them fearfully.

"Come! We must return to the castle. We are almost there. Follow me," he said.

He pushed aside some low branches and Robert gasped. Rising from the green forest floor, partly camouflaged by paint and foliage, were the ramparts of a fortified village. Right in front of them was a drawbridge across the moat. Two archers stood waiting to close it.

Robert and Alice walked across and into the secret, hidden place.

"It's amazing," said Alice.

"Welcome to Wellhagh," said Sir Elias. "In your day you will know it as Wellow."

"I know it," said Alice. "We are from Newark. Wellow is the village on the way to the Center Parcs holiday village in Sherwood Forest where we go on holiday sometimes. It's the pretty village with the triangular green and the enormous maypole."

"Who is the King of England at this time?" asked Robert.

"King John," said Sir Elias. "He comes to Sherwood forest to his hunting lodge from time to time."

"Of course. The ruins of that are still there in our time near my friend's house in a village called Clipstone. It's near Mansfield, I've seen it," said Robert smiling.

"What year are we in?" said Alice.

"Eleven hundred and ninety-eight," said Sir Elias.

"That's almost a hundred years before the time we travelled to when we met the Sheriff at the beginning of this quest. He wasn't an old man though," said Robert.

"No, he wouldn't be. He has chosen to suspend his ageing," said Sir Elias. "Once you are a powerful enough Time Regent you can choose to do that. Good Regents generally only do it for a serious reason, to help in a quest. But evil Regents do it to suit their own greed."

"Sounds exciting but I think I'd miss my friends and stuff," said Robert. "I hope we don't have to make that kind of choice ever."

Sir Elias looked at Robert seriously for a minute before his face creased into a smile.

"Come on," he said.

They wandered through the bustling village, past rows of wooden houses each surrounded by small strips of land where vegetables grew. A terrier barked in the miller's enclosure and sweet smells of honey mead and herb punch drifted out from the brewer's house. Children played happily with wooden toys or fought each other with miniature quarter staffs and swords.

"The forest gives us everything. The hunt hereabouts is the best in England. We eat grouse, hare, deer and duck. The trees give us wood for our homes, our harps and our bows and charcoal for our ovens and forges," said Sir Elias.

Two boys stopped playing and stared at Robert and Alice.

"How is it that we are so visible out of our own time?" said Alice.

"You did not wish it on yourselves?" said Sir Elias.

Alice and Robert shook their heads.

"I didn't know we could," said Alice.

"Oh, yes," said Sir Elias. "Once your power has increased sufficiently over many quests you will be able to turn it on and off at will. If, as you say, it is without your consent, then it has been willed upon you until the quest is finished by another Regent, and one with great powers. The Regent must think that visibility to the common man may make you more vulnerable."

Robert and Alice glanced at one another.

"The Sheriff, I bet," said Robert.

Alice pursed her lips and nodded slowly.

"We'll have to make the best of it," she said.

"There are some advantages. At least we can join in medieval life properly."

They walked on towards another wooden dwelling with a goatskin door.

"This is the favourite place for bowmen to look in their spare time and if they have spare silver to spend," said Sir Elias. "It is William the fletcher's. He is my personal bowyer too. I think you two may need some weaponry from here if we are to defeat our enemies."

"What does a fletcher do?" asked Alice.

"A fletcher forms the arrows that we shoot from Saxon flat bows or sometimes the new longbows," said Sir Elias.

A thin man with friendly brown eyes ducked through the doorway.

Robert thought there was something familiar about this man.

"Sire," said William the fletcher.

"Perhaps you would allow our friends to choose from your special collection?" said Sir Elias.

William bowed graciously. He was dressed in a woollen tunic of reddish brown with a linen undershirt showing at the neck and cuffs. Bulging leather pouches dangled from his buckled belt.

"William's skills have given fellow Time Regents the means to fell so many of our enemies, as did his father. And as his sons and daughters will continue to do so after him," said Sir Elias.

"Indeed so, Sire," said William. "Welcome to my home and my workshop."

Tree trunks stood in tidy rows against the wooden perimeter of the front enclosure. Different sections had been trimmed and separated.

"This is yew," said William, brushing his hand lovingly along the wood. "The secret of the power of yew lies in correctly combining heart wood with sapwood. The heartwood is very strong and the sapwood is elastic. If worked together with skill, the two woods in the same bow will send arrows far and yet return the bow to straightness after each shot. How kind it is that one variety of tree should deliver us both powers."

Alice ran her hand over the woods.

"Take care, young lady," said William. The yew tree guards its secret with strong poison. Unskilled bowyers can expect to die at twenty or at most twenty-five years of age if they do not take precautions."

Alice recoiled her hand. The fletcher walked over to a collection of pots and bottles.

"Here are my protectors," he said. "Beeswax and linseed oil. Without a protective covering with these, I and our archers would slowly poison ourselves to death."

"Clever," said Robert. "And these must be the feathers for the arrows."

"Indeed," came a younger voice. "Peacock or goose."

A boy emerged from the house. He wore a separate loose yellow hood over his red tunic. The pointed linpipe end of the hood trailed over one shoulder. He had the same hazel eyes as the fletcher and a mop of curly blonde hair poking out at the edges of his hood. Like most of the people in this forest village, his smooth skin was browned by their outdoor life.

"This is my son, Thomas," said William. "He has the makings of a fine squire. Pity he keeps forgetting to bring me bluebells for the glue to stick the arrowheads to the shafts!"

The older man gave his son an affectionate punch on the arm.

The boy grinned and shook hands with Robert. He bowed to Alice, kissing her hand.

"Have we met somewhere before?" said Alice.

Robert noticed she was blushing slightly. He looked carefully at this confident young man.

"No," said Thomas. Then he whispered softly in Alice's ear just loudly enough for Robert to hear. "Unless you have met some of my descendents through time?"

Robert knew that this young man must be a time traveller too.

"Show them your specials," said Sir Elias stepping forward. He put his arm around Thomas affectionately. "Our friends here are going to need the very best."

They went inside. William lead them to a back chamber. He took a silver key from around his neck and unlocked a long, heavy chest. He reached in and lifted out a selection of bows and quivers. The shiny spun flax of the new bow strings was perfectly fitted. He measured one against Robert and gave it to him. He took a slightly smaller one for Alice.

"Wow! It feels fantastic!" murmured Robert. "Much lighter and smoother than the ones we've used in archery lessons at Center Parcs."

"How is your shooting?" asked Thomas.

"He's brilliant," said Alice.

"Actually, you're even better than me," said Robert. "I'm probably better with a sword though."

"Oh, ho! Confidence is good, but I think you will need a little tutoring to get you good enough to match the foes we seek. These are the finest bows ever crafted and with just a little practice, I think you will be good enough," said Sir Elias.

"And here are the arrows," said William. He handed them both a quiver of arrows crowned with beautiful peacock feathers. "Guard these well. You may need them to save your life very soon, if what Sir Elias has talked of comes to pass."

As he spoke they heard the sound of hunting horns.

The two men stiffened.

"The signal," said William.

"Come, friends," said Sir Elias. "To the safety of the castle keep! Enemies approach."

6

The Castle in the Forest

"May I go too, father?" said Thomas. "I am ready."

William looked sadly at his son.

"Very well. But stay close to the master. Elias may need you. Take this," he said.

He opened a wooden cupboard. He passed a sword to his son.

"This sword has been the defender of our family for many generations," said William the fletcher. "Like the Foliot family, our ancestors came across to England with William the Conqueror in ten hundred and sixty-six, over a century ago. This sword came with them. I have always known that one day it would be used again. Some day soon you will need to remember all that I have taught you."

Solemnly, he passed it to his son.

"How cool is that?" murmured Robert. "Wish we had one of those hidden in some old wardrobe in my family."

Thomas was silent. He was shaking slightly.

"Thank you, father," he said. "I will always honour our family's duties, with my life if necessary."

"Ahem," coughed Sir Elias. "We must depart I'm afraid."

He bowed to William and ducked out of the fletcher's home. The others followed, across the triangular village green and up a track towards the motte and bailey of the compact castle. More warning blasts from hunting horns echoed from the deep forest all around them.

They ran through the gatehouse and began to

climb the steps inside the keep.

"Glad I keep fit!" puffed Robert.

He adjusted his new quiver. The soft leather felt comfortable across his back but it was difficult to hold the bow up high enough to stop it bumping the stone steps.

"Keep up, slow coach!" shouted Alice from in front. She leapt up the steps two at a time.

Robert could feel a cooler breeze from above diluting the warmer air in the stairwell. They went past the doorways of several castle levels where the fire-lit chambers gave a tempting glimpse of the medieval world within. Robert even saw the balustrades of a minstrel gallery and what looked like the great hall below.

At the top, the stairs opened onto the narrow ledge around the perimeter of the small, square castle. Elias led them past the archers stationed along the battlements. Horns still sounded, some near and others further away in the forest. They climbed a short circular stairway to the top of one of the corner towers. There was barely room for all of them to squeeze out at the very top.

The view was breathtaking.

"You can see the whole forest," breathed Robert. "Like a falcon would. The tops of the trees look like a patchwork quilt."

I can't believe how high we are," said Alice. "Don't push. I don't fancy falling off from up here."

Sir Elias was listening to the horns and staring beyond the village in the direction of the point of the triangular green.

"Someone approaches from Nottingham," he said, pointing.

Thomas nodded. Robert could just see movement where the trees were thinner.

"Oh, where is John when I need him?" whispered Elias to himself.

"My Lord, come quickly!" someone shouted up the stairwell.

Elias slipped down the steep stairs, almost sliding down the iron banister, with the ease of someone who has done it many times since boyhood. A squire handed him a scroll.

"It is the Sheriff himself," he panted. "One of his men is in the courtyard. He brings you this scroll. Our men ambushed him and brought him here. They are in position to attack the Sheriff's party but await your command."

"That's very bold of the Sheriff," said Elias. "He should know by now that his clumsy soldiers with their heavy chain mail and their colourful flags are easy targets for the nimble bowmen of the forest. Why would he come to us like this?" He opened the scroll and read the short message. His face went white and his eyes hardened with hatred.

"He has taken John!" he breathed. "He has him imprisoned as his hostage."

"Where, Sire? In Nottingham Castle?" said Thomas.

"No. In a much more deadly prison. My dearest friend lies wounded in a Time Cage."

Robert and Alice looked at each other. Robert knew why Alice looked so afraid. Time Cages were suspended outside the reach of normal mortals, locked in a secret chasm, probably deep in a far away galaxy between the pathways of time itself.

Instinctively, he felt for the jewel Time Trigger just in case they needed to escape. It was still nestling in his blazer pocket. He knew it might be possible to focus their powers enough to time travel without holding a Trigger. But it would be easier with one and he didn't want to risk it.

Sir Elias looked at Alice and Robert.

"This Sheriff seeks an exchange," he said. "He will return my friend if I hand over you two."

Robert felt Alice's hand slip into his arm.

"And what do you plan to do?" said Robert aggressively.

Sir Elias smiled.

"I admire your courage, Robert. I can see that one day you will be the mighty Regent the ballads have foretold. Do you think that I would betray you?" he said.

"I'm not sure," said Robert.

"We don't really know who is on our side and who is against us," said Alice. "And we don't know why we have been summoned to this place and time."

"I realise that," said Sir Elias. "And now I understand what has gone wrong. John was protecting you. He was about to warn you and explain your destiny I should think. But the Sheriff and his allies intercepted and took him before he could fulfil his duty."

"We have had nobody looking after us," said Alice.

"Oh, yes you have," said Sir Elias. "Since your births, the High Regents have watched you. We have seen visions of what must be, revealed to us by the Spirits of Time in the Shells of Destiny. We have long known that you would have to face the Sheriff one day, when the masks resurfaced."

"What masks?" said Robert and Alice together.

Sir Elias looked over the battlements into the forest. Several narrow columns of smoke were now rising from the canopy of leaves and drifting gently in the evening breeze.

"The Sheriff has made camp for the night I see," he said. "He is in no hurry."

"Will you not attack?" said Thomas. "Your men could easily. .."

"No," said Elias. "Not yet. I need to think. Come to my chamber. I have something you should see."

They followed him down the steps and onto a landing lit by flaming torches. Elias took a heavy key from his belt and unlocked a door. The fire in the stone fireplace within spluttered and cracked. A table was littered with the remains of a simple meal of bread and meat and wine. Rich tapestries hung across two of the walls. A high bed stood on a platform at one end, dwarfed in the huge room.

Sir Elias walked across to a smaller door and unlocked this one.

"Wait here, Thomas, and stand guard," he said.

Thomas checked his sword was running smoothly in its scabbard.

Elias lifted down a wall torch and disappeared into the dark interior. He stooped under the oak mantel above the doorway and down a few steps, followed in the torchlight by his jagged shadow on the rough stone wall of the inner cave.

The others followed cautiously.

"Have you ever been here before?" said Robert to Thomas as he walked past him.

"No, never," said Thomas. "But my father has spoken of the secrets of this sacred place."

7

Little John

Robert followed Alice down the steps.

"We are quite safe in here," said Sir Elias. He lifted a great wooden beam into iron brackets to bar the door and walked around the cave lighting more torches. "Not even a Time Regent could easily penetrate these walls unbidden. Sit, please."

He gestured them to each take a seat on one of the six high backed arm chairs that were positioned around a tall, round table. Something was hidden under a cloth that projected from the table like an iceberg. Each chair was lined with furs and silk and was very comfortable. Robert noticed elf-like carvings dancing across the arms and down the legs and etched on the front of the table was the circle sign again.

Sir Elias stood behind the table. In the torch light, his face was a tapestry of terrifying shadows. Robert was reminded of other experienced Time Regents he had met with Alice, like Eidor the Shaman who had helped them in France, and the beautiful Lady Godiva who had steered them safely away from treacherous Vikings in another quest. There was also something that reminded him of the Indian chief Massasoit. They all had the same powerful eyes that glowed hypnotically with the promise of eternal stories from the corridors of time, even of ages yet unknown.

"What is this place?" said Alice.

"I come to this cave to use the Shell of Destiny just as my father did, and my descendents will," said Sir

Elias. "Usually, we are with the chief guardian, Little John. The shell is entrusted to him, but any powerful Time Regent is able to use it. Thomas' father has been here too. His family are Time Squires; travellers without whose faithful service the High Regents could not succeed in their battles against evil. This secret place is only known to us."

"And are you Robin Hood?" said Robert.

The tall man threw back his head and laughed.

"Who is Robin Hood? As I said before, the name is a cloak. And not only for the protection of my people when we are forced to defend ourselves. There is a greater purpose. Robin Hood is a myth to hide the true identities of those who guard the masks. If he were one person, perhaps I could say I was he. But if I can, my friend, so can you. You too are Robin Hood."

Robert felt his heart beating faster. Alice was grinning at him.

"That makes me Maid Marion, I suppose," she said.

"Yes, if you like," said Elias. "Like Robin Hood, the Lady Marion is just a performance name for an important role that must be played on the stage of time. You both will have to make choices some day soon. You must decide whether to leave your birth life and take up an eternal role as High Regent, as John has done. Unfortunately, so has the Sheriff. It is up to each of us to decide within ourselves when the time is right which path to follow."

"And the masks?" said Alice.

"Ah, those," sighed Elias. "Let me show you."

He swept the cloth from the table to reveal a giant conch shell. This was not the first time Robert and Alice had seen one of these. Its pale salmon colour was speckled with glittery sand and edged with a delicate pure white frill that framed the mirrored interior.

Elias sprinkled some powders around them on the floor and picked up the shell in both his hands. He began to draw a square in the air above him. Very soon the space he had defined became a screen of shimmering glass. Elias closed his eyes and began to chant. The cave smelt strongly now from the powdered spices. Robert felt drowsy.

The shimmering screen flickered to life.

"It looks like a battle," said Alice. "I can see people falling from horses and being stabbed."

"The year is ten hundred and sixty six," said Elias.

"The Battle of Hastings," said Robert.

"Exactly," said Elias. "Look closely." A man rode into view. "That is my ancestor who came across with William. He carries a valuable parcel inside his cloak. He was a guardian of the masks and brought them with him for safety. They are quite small and plain, save for three jewels on each. On the first mask there is a sapphire, an emerald and a diamond. On the second are an amethyst, garnet and opal. The jewels were bound to the masks with silver from the silver mines of Saxony by ancient Regents. They have grown in strength and are thought to be the most powerful Time Triggers in existence. With them, a time traveller could safely visit anywhere in any time, even far out in space in distant galaxies. They would not run the risk of being marooned as one of us would if we were to misuse an ordinary Time Trigger for our own selfish purposes instead of as part of a quest."

"What happened to these masks?" said Alice.

"According to ballads past down the generations, they lie secretly buried somewhere in the Sherwood, placed there by my ancestor after several attempts by evil Regents to acquire them. The exact location was never passed on, in order to protect the masks. Yet still they come to find them, the evil ones, growing more cunning all the time. And they will not stop down the centuries, especially the Sheriff of Nottingham, the arch enemy of Robin Hood. He knows more than ordinary mortals but I do not think he fully comprehends who the guardian Regents are. The Sheriff is deeply suspicious of me. He knows there is a connection with Robin Hood and the masks and he will get closer. And he has allies."

"So, Robin Hood, the robber in the wood, is a myth that has covered the identities of different Time Regents who guard the masks over many centuries," said Alice, thoughtfully.

"Exactly so," said Elias. "And the deeds attributed to Robin Hood occur throughout Nottinghamshire and Yorkshire. Apart from our stronghold in Sherwood Forest, the Foliot family has land in Barnsdale Forest and a chapel in Yorkshire. In your history books there is so much dispute over the identity of the so called Robin Hood. Your historians try to prove Robin was this man or that. In fact he was not one man but many. He represents our struggle to keep the power of the masks from falling into the grasp of those who would use it for greed and power."

"So where do we come in?" said Robert.

"It is prophesied that the masks are about to surface again after nearly a millennium," said Sir Elias. "Look at the screen. A disturbance to the forest in your time is a threat to the safety of the masks."

The flickering screen blurred and became more focussed again.

"Whatever is that tractor thing?" said Robert.

"It is a machine of your time," said Elias.

"It's a JCB digger, excavating ground in a forest," said Robert.

"This very forest," said Elias. "It is only a very short time before you must fulfil your destiny as it has been foretold and prevent the masks from falling into the hands of the most evil of Time Regents. When the time is right, you will know where they are and protect them."

"But if you have seen this," said Alice. "Why can't you do it?"

"It is not my destiny," said Sir Elias. "I know in my soul that I no longer have the powers to travel far into the future. My job is now to keep this village strong and the myth of Robin Hood alive. My own descendents you have yet to meet, for they too must fight off the Sheriff. My time on earth is almost over. Only you who are born in the right time can attain sufficient power to defeat the evil that will try to snatch the masks. He must be lurking in your time too, biding his time. He will have time travelled there even if he has not lived on through the centuries like John."

"In our age the Sheriff of Nottingham does not have a very important job," said Robert. "That's sounds more like the politicians. They make all the decisions."

"Then that is almost certainly where the enemy will hide himself, camouflaged like a speckled snake on stony ground. But beware. Trust no-one. The Sheriff will have evil friends. They have learned many new powers. They like to capture Time Regents and drawn strength from them. Some who were once good have turned to their wickedness and joined them. Beware. Like chameleons, evil Regents can change themselves to blend in. They might occupy a less obvious position of power over you."

Alice gasped.

"Could they be a woman?" she said.

"Of course," said Elias. "In fact the shadow of a woman crosses the picture of the shell many times. I do not know if she is friend or foe but she is involved somehow and it is your destiny to meet, I think. At first I had the feeling she might be an incarnation of the Lady Marion. But I am no longer sure."

Robert looked at Alice. Suddenly he knew what she was thinking.

"Miss Gilbert?" he said.

Alice nodded.

Sir Elias started shaking. He closed his eyes and the shell screen changed again. Someone was moaning in pain. The screen was dark. Robert shuddered and started to sweat. He could sense the evil. He could even smell the stench of the dead.

As the screen cleared slightly, they could see a big man hunched in the corner of a grimy dungeon.

"John!" breathed Elias. "He is dying from his wounds. He will be left there to rot in his Time Cage."

"Is he the Little John of the Robin Hood legend?" said Alice.

"Of course," said Elias. "He is the gentle giant who appears always at Robin's side. We joke and call him little because he is so big. He is probably the noblest of all Time Regents and the chief guardian of the masks, for he has never chosen a mortal life, like the rest of us. We normal Regents help him down the generations. He lives on and stays with each generation."

"Can he ever die?" said Robert.

"Oh, yes. He is still mortal in that way, if he is killed by weaponry. But his body will not age."

"Is Little John his real name?" said Alice.

"No," said Elias. "He is known as Reynolde Greenleaf in your famous Robin Hood poem, called the Gest. His real name is John Reynolds."

Robert nearly choked.

"My God! He has been guarding us all this time. But I would never have suspected..." said Robert.

"Mr Reynolds!" gasped Alice. "Of course. It all makes sense. I can't believe we didn't see the clues."

8

The Seventh Jewel

"Perhaps at last he has been struck down and imprisoned by one too powerful for any of us to repel," said Sir Elias.

"Can't we save him?" said Alice. There was panic and fear in her voice.

"I don't know how strong you are," said Elias. "But you must not prejudice the saving of the masks. John would not want that. Your duty lies there first. I fear it is all a trap. If you try to rescue John, you may be captured yourself and that would leave the masterminds of this plan to grab the masks when they surface."

"There must be another way to save John. Who else can we call upon to help?" said Alice.

"Friar Tuck?" said Robert grinning.

"Don't joke, Robert," said Alice. "This is serious."

"But I'm not joking," said Robert. "We've already met him, I think, in another century."

Alice frowned at him.

"Of course!" she said. "The fat monk."

"And he had a little helper, one Thomas of Wellow..." said Robert, raising his eyebrows. He waited for Alice to work it out.

"He did look like Thomas and William the fletcher I suppose," said Alice.

Alice quickly described their meeting earlier.

"That's it!" said Sir Elias. "This Thomas you speak of will be the descendent of the Squires who serve me so well. You time travelled to my future when my own grandchildren are probably the guardians with John a century from now. I have underestimated you two. You have powerful secrets and worthy friends. I think that is where you should go for help. That is the time setting for the next chapter of this quest. But you have also been seen by the Sheriff in that time. Tell me this, something I have meant to ask you. How did you travel here originally?"

Robert slowly brought out the jewel from his inside blazer pocket. It was wrapped in his handkerchief. As he unwrapped it, Sir Elias stepped back in surprise.

"The seventh jewel! The ruby. I had thought that was a myth!" he said. "You have not yet seen the masks, have you? When you do, you will see that this little gem matches the three that are laid across the top of each of them in size and shape. Its existence has long been doubted by the High Regents. It seems it fell into the wrong hands long ago. Well, well! Our enemies do play for high stakes if they lure you with that!"

Just then, they heard a knocking on the door.

Sir Elias moved a tiny cover from a spy hole three quarters of the way up and peered through.

"It is Thomas, but he looks worried," he said as he drew back the huge oak beam that locked them in.

"Sire! Thanks be to the Holy Lady," he gasped. "It is him... the Sheriff. He approaches through the great hall as I speak. Somehow he transported himself within the castle itself. He is alone but he is killing all who challenge him!"

Sir Elias turned to Robert and Alice.

"You must go. This is not your battle, not yet. I will dispatch him." He put an arm across Thomas' shoulders. "... with my trusted Squire."

Thomas drew his heavy sword.

"We will go," said Robert. He took Alice's hand. "Goodbye, Sir Elias and good luck."

Alice squeezed Robert's hand and they closed their eyes.

"To the fourteenth century then?" said Alice.

"No," said Robert. "I've got a better idea. Let's go home to the twenty first century to start with. I want to examine Mr Reynolds' room again."

Alice opened her eyes again.

"Mmm. . . ."

"Look, Alice, we've got to agree here or I dread to think what will become of us in the Time Tunnel if you try to get us to one century while I'm concentrating on some other time."

"O.K," said Alice. "You're probably right. Anyhow, I'm starving and I'm not too sure about the roast boar burgers we're likely to get served in the Greenwood."

Robert grinned at her.

Within seconds, everything went white. Robert felt the suction of time travel that sometimes made him worry his heart or brain would be pulled out. Light seared through him and he felt the voices of a thousand years of souls singing in both his ears. It was way better than the fastest, meanest rollercoaster ride.

Their school was in darkness.

"Let's go back to Mr Reynold's room," said Alice. "We need some clues to try and get him out. Time Cages are almost impossible to locate. It could be in any galaxy in any time."

They reached the door to his office.

"It's locked," said Robert. "But I have a way. .."

He reached into his trouser pocket and brought out his special penknife. Alice looked at him suspiciously, with one eyebrow lifted.

"Hmm. One of your little gadgets?" she said, grinning.

"But of course," said Robert. "Keep a look out and give me a couple of secs...."

He fiddled in the keyhole with his lock-picker. Police sirens sounded in the street outside and the flashing blue light sent a strobe of violet through the windows between the shadows of the dark corridor. The noise faded into the distance. The town was quiet again. Robert glanced at his watch. It was four in the morning when most people would be in their beds.

"There!" said Robert.

The lock clicked and he turned the door handle. He felt for the light switch.

"No!" shouted Alice. "No lights. Someone might see."

She glanced down the corridor both ways. "There's enough light from the street lamps outside."

"And it's full moon," said Robert. He ran his hands creepily up Alice's spine.

"Stop it, idiot!" breathed Alice. "Concentrate! Look around for something that might help us find Little John."

"Ouch!" said Robert, banging his knee. "This drawer is open. Oh! The rest have gone. There were more scrolls in here before" He patted the parchment still safe inside his blazer. "Good job I borrowed this one, I think."

"And everywhere is tidy," said Alice. "Even the blood stain has gone. And the wall charts. Someone's been cleaning up the evidence."

She brushed her fingers across the key pad of the computer.

"Just a minute," said Robert.

He pressed the button for the computer screen and it flickered into life.

Alice read the message.

"Robert, Alice, dance?" she said. She pressed the scroll down key automatically. "Oh. That wasn't all of it."

"It wasn't?" said Robert. "I didn't have time to check before."

ROBERT
ALICE
DANCE
ELVES
TUCK

"Hmm. Still no wiser," said Alice. "But it does mention a possible connection to Friar Tuck. I think that's where we have to go for help."

"Did you hear something?" said Robert. "Rustling?"

"No but I can smell burning," said Alice. "And that's smoke coming under the door."

"Someone's started a fire!" said Robert. They heard a high pitched laugh. "They're trying to kill us."

9

Foul Smoke and Venom

"Quick! Out of the window," said Alice.

She flipped the inside lock on the window catch. It was stuck.

Foul smelling smoke was filling the room now. Robert started to cough.

"This isn't ordinary smoke," he spluttered. "There's a nasty chemical smell about it" He stumbled, trying not to be sick. "We have to get away from this stuff before it kills us."

Alice pushed the window with all her strength.

"It's open!" she said. She pulled herself onto the ledge. "Come on!"

Covering his mouth and nose with his hands, Robert lunged towards the open ground floor window after Alice. He levered himself over the sill after her and dropped down onto the gravel of the enclosed staff garden. The gargoyles on the silent water fountain stared back at them. Alice and Robert coughed and spluttered.

"We're a bit stuck, out in this quad with all the doors locked," said Alice. "There's no way back in."

"Well at least we're safe from the fire and those deadly fumes," said Robert, still choking. "Maybe we'll just have to time travel out of here. Someone wants us dead."

Flames were pouring through the window of Mr Reynold's office now. The window of the glass door opposite cracked and smashed into a myriad of sparkling shards. Robert and Alice ducked, covering their faces protectively.

"Was that the heat that broke the glass?" said Alice.

"No. It was my sword!" said a woman's voice.

Miss Gilbert stepped through the jagged remains of the glass door. She was no longer dressed in her modern checked jacket and skirt. Now she wore long white and gold nunnery robes. She had a black silk veil over her white wimpole.

"Ah!" said Alice. "I didn't think you were going to give me a very high mark for my French test, but I didn't expect you to kill me."

"Do you think you are clever?" cackled Miss Gilbert. "There is no time to joke, Alice. I am fed up with watching you two. Prepare to die. I have had the signal."

"Teachers are supposed to look after their pupils," said Alice.

"Ha! Don't start preaching to me. I am the prioress here," said Miss Gilbert.

"People who work for the church are supposed to be good too," said Alice.

The Prioress laughed.

"Where did you get that idea, my dear?" she said.

Alice looked cross now.

"Your words are venom," said Alice. "You are an imposter, a Time Regent who has been tempted to swap over to evil. You have taken Mr Reynolds and imprisoned him in a Time Cage, haven't you?"

Miss Gilbert, the Prioress, smiled slowly and raised her sword.

"Are you the brains behind everything or have you a master?" said Alice.

The Prioress stepped towards them, her face twisting into a mask of hatred.

Robert was ready. He had already managed to slide an arrow from his back while Alice distracted the woman. He slid it into the groove on the bow. He knew Alice had seen him. He edged around the quadrangle towards the broken door as Alice taunted the thin woman further.

"You do have a master don't you? You are too stupid to have worked it all out. Where have you taken Mr Reynolds or should I call him Little John?" said Alice.

"I answer to no-one! Only the deepest trance could find John," said the Prioress. "There is no-one amongst your forest friends who might know the way to do that. And anyway, you will never see any of them again!"

The Prioress charged forwards.

Robert let his arrow fly.

"Arghh!" screamed the Prioress.

Robert's arrow landed in her shoulder. She dropped the sword and fell onto her knees.

"Quick! Take my hand, Alice," he said.

Alice stooped and picked up the sword. Robert pulled her towards the door.

"You will not get far," said the Prioress taking rasping breaths. Blood seeped through her robes. "If I die, the Sheriff will get you. He will never let you claim the masks."

Alice turned to look at the woman.

"Ah, so you do have a master," said Alice.

"Bah! He is not my master," spat the Prioress. "We are equals. He needs my knowledge of Time Lore and I need his armies of power. He cannot extend his time travelling powers even using roving Time Tunnels, not as I can in one of my trances. The Sheriff could not operate a Time Cage and send it to the edges of time. If I die, Little John will perish. What a terrible fate out there in his cage. Shame. He was a handsome man. A little quiet perhaps, but popular in the staff room of your school."

Robert could feel Alice's muscles tighten. She lifted the sword and pointed it at the woman.

"You would not have the courage to finish me off," cackled the Prioress.

"Don't waste time on her," said Robert. "She's not worth it. Let's go."

"We don't need you," said Alice. "I think I know who will help us and we're off to see him now. Little John left us a message."

"A message? Impossible. He was unconscious after I wounded him. I checked the room. . ."

"Maybe he wasn't quite as injured as you thought," said Alice. "Did you check the computer?"

"It wasn't on, was it. . . ?" The smile vanished from the woman's face.

"Alice, let's go," said Robert.

"Goodbye," said Alice.

"I will have my revenge on you!" shouted the Prioress after them as they climbed carefully through what remained of the jagged glass door. "I will kill Robin Hood once and for all!"

Her croaky voice faded away as they ran through the staff room in the moonlight and opened the door onto the inner corridor. Traces of the stinking smoke lingered here and there. Robert pulled his shirt over his mouth as they ran on and out of the school. They didn't stop running until they reached the bus station along the main road in the centre of Newark.

There were only a few people loitering on benches, but the all night café was open.

"Let's get something to eat," said Alice.

Robert looked at her. Her uniform was dirty and her dishevelled blond hair settled chaotically around her shoulders above her quiver of peacock arrows. With the back of her hand that held the long bow, she wiped a stray hair from her dirt-streaked face. In the other hand, she clutched Miss Gilbert's sword. She looked fierce and pretty at the same time. Robert grinned.

"You look like something out of a horror movie," he said. "Kind of nice though. Like a mad pirate goddess."

"Thanks," said Alice. She frowned at him. "And funnily enough, apart from your school stuff, you look like you've just been to a fancy dress party."

"Good job there's no-one around, eh?" said Robert. "Can I buy you a coke and a burger?"

"Chocolate, please," said Alice. "I need energy quickly!"

Inside the café they sat down with their snack and ate hungrily.

"When we've finished this, we'd better get back to see the fat monk, hadn't we?" said Robert.

"Yep, and I hope he knows what the message means about the elf dance thing on the computer," said Alice.

"What message would that be then?" came a deep voice from behind them.

Alice and Robert jumped up.

"Now will you give me the sign?" said the man.

10

The Fat Monk

From the shadows in the far corner of the café, the monk they had seen earlier stepped out. His bald head reflected the light from the lamp post outside. Robert smelt the herby odour again.

Robert held up the palm of his hand where he had drawn the ring and the little lines of light with a biro.

"Friar Tuck, I presume?" said Robert.

The man bowed in acknowledgement.

"This time, I know you, Sire," said the monk. "My Lady. .."

He took Alice's hand and kissed it.

"I must apologise for being a little hostile when we last met, but I needed to be sure. I live in dangerous times and it is never wise to trust anyone on the first meeting."

"It's quite alright," said Alice. "We understand. Especially since we met our friend the Prioress."

Alarm flared across the monk's face.

"It's O.K," said Robert. "I shot her."

The monk looked at Robert in surprise.

"And is she... dead?" he said.

"Um, I don't think so," said Robert. "I deliberately aimed for her shoulder. But she's quite badly injured."

"Hmm. Shoulder wounds can be very severe, even fatal. Her powers will certainly be weakened for a while," said the monk thoughtfully.

He looked up at them. His round brown eyes were wise and friendly.

"From what I overheard just now, you want to ask me about dancing?" he said.

"How much do you know about what has happened?" said Alice.

"After your last visit I spoke to my real master, Sir Richard of the Lea. Richard Foliot to you. I think you have met his grandfather, Elias. We used the Shell of Destiny to help us see what had transpired and where you were. Sir Richard is under siege at his castle but I entered secretly using the special Wellow tunnels," said the monk. "The Sheriff was one step ahead of us I am ashamed to say. We had not expected you so soon. But unknown to us, he or someone had slipped you the seventh jewel and created a powerful Time Tunnel to whisk you two into his clutches well before the masks were due to surface, hoping to prevent the prophecy from coming true."

"What prophecy?" said Alice.

"That you two, the Robin Hood and Lady Marion of the now, would find the masks, the mightiest of Time Triggers, and become the most powerful Time Regents ever known."

"I like the sound of all that power," said Robert.

Alice punched him on the arm.

"Let's concentrate on the quest, shall we?" she said, frowning at him.

"Only joking...My Lady," said Robert, winking.

"Friar Tuck, can I ask you something?" said Alice.

"Of course," said the monk.

"We thought you meant the Sheriff when you talked about your master with Thomas of Wellow," said Robert.

He noticed the monk's fleeting look of fear.

"How is it that the Sheriff of Nottingham hired you as his cook if you are working for the Robin Hood team?" said Alice.

"My Lady, you are as intelligent as you are beautiful," said Friar Tuck. "A good question. The answer is simple. I am a double agent. The Sheriff doesn't know who I really am. Well he didn't. He may do by now, although the brains behind our enemy is the Prioress of Kirklees, who, from what you say, is now considerably weakened. She is the one who can time travel deep into the outer reaches of our universe. In fact, I bet it was her who slipped you the seventh jewel, not the Sheriff."

"That would make sense," said Robert. "The Sheriff did seem to think we were a little early, almost as if he wasn't quite expecting us yet."

"But he'd have had you killed anyway," said the monk.

"Where has the Prioress sent Little John's Time Cage?" said Alice.

Friar Tuck was looking across at the café counter.

"Ah, well, I think we may be able to find him together," he said. "What are those delicious looking round, sticky things?"

Robert followed his gaze.

"Dough-nuts," said Robert. "Dough filled with jam and covered in sugar."

"Sugar?" said Friar Tuck. "Mmmm. I know of it from my travels. In my own time my sweet tooth has to make do with honey. May I...?"

Alice and Robert grinned at him.

"I wonder which of his remaining teeth is his sweet one?" whispered Robert.

Alice pulled out her purse.

"A dough-nut, please. Anything else Friar Tuck?" she asked.

The woman behind the counter looked up from her magazine. She stared at the three of them suspiciously.

"Well, let me see... said the monk.

He chose a bag of wine gums, a rather stale looking chicken sandwich and a packet of cheese and onion crisps.

"These will be lovely with a glass of mead for my supper I should think," he said, forcing them into a pouch on his belt and rubbing his fat belly affectionately.

Alice paid for them, smiling as much as possible at the woman behind the counter who shrugged her shoulders.

"Young people!" she muttered, before picking up her magazine again and completely ignoring them.

They sat down on the benches at the far end of the dingy café.

"Now let us make plans," said Friar Tuck. "This is our council of war. Sir Richard sent me to help you. Tell me everything you know."

Robert smiled to himself. It was a strange place for a council of war but perhaps they were more hidden here from the all seeing eyes of the Sheriff of Nottingham and the Prioress.

"What do you make of Little John's computer message?" said Alice.

"Oh, ho! Our friend knows only too well that I have knowledge of the medicinal herbs that grow in our great forest. With some of these, I can enter the spirit world and travel into space in my trances. We call it the elf dance to conceal its true power. If we return to my century I will show you. Together we may be able to rescue John. Now is the time. While the Prioress' powers are weak, the field that keeps the Time Cage suspended will also be less strong. Come. Let us use the seventh jewel and make a Time Tunnel back to my forest at the close of the thirteenth century and the dawn of the fourteenth century. Shall we say the year twelve hundred and ninety-nine? I think that's where I came from."

"You don't really need a Time Trigger do you, to time travel? Your powers are so great already aren't they?" said Alice.

"Actually, although I can project my mind to other galaxies in one of my trances, I do not often move my body. Too much lard on it perhaps!" joked the monk. "Sir Richard Foliot had to help me by tapping into the strength of the Shell of Destiny to get me here. You two have greater powers than do we. You have been expected. It is your destiny to remain Time Regents and to become legends, unless you reject that choice of course."

Robert shivered slightly. He glanced at Alice. She looked worried too. All this talk of being such powerful time travellers and giving up their ordinary lives made Robert nervous. He liked things the way they were, having adventures and coming back to the comfort of his twenty-first century life as a normal boy most of the time. He liked watching Nottingham Forest football games and playing on his X-box and watching DVDs. Being a kind of super hero sounded a bit too much like hard work. He'd never really thought about what he'd like to be when he was older. For a tiny, worrying second, he wondered what his destiny would be.

11

Sheriff's Hostage

Friar Tuck tapped Robert on the arm.

"Stop day dreaming, my young friend. There is much to do. Pick up your weapons, for I think they will be needed in the hours and days to come. Take my hand and let us time travel," he said.

Robert took out the jewel Time Trigger. They closed their eyes. Robert concentrated on seeing again the Sherwood Forest of twelve hundred and ninety-nine. Amid the whiteness and brilliance of the Time Tunnel, he could hear the fluttering of the wind in the oak leaves and smell the sweet dampness of the mossy forest floor.

But as the speed of the time travel slowed, there were other sounds. Men shouted and horses whinnied.

Robert opened his eyes.

They were back.

"Oops! I think perhaps we could have done better with our geography and been less obvious," said Friar Tuck.

"Well, well! So you could not resist us. I admire your courage in the face of war," said the Sheriff of Nottingham.

This time he was not showing his white teeth in a cheesy smile. Now he was glaring at Robert and Alice with malicious eyes.

"Do you bring weapons?" said the Sheriff. "Ha! I don't think you will be able to draw much blood with that broadsword. It takes my pages and my squires many years of training, some from the age of seven or eight years, until they are knights at twenty one."

"Perhaps," said Alice defiantly. "But then again we are the ones who prophesy predicts will beat you all. We are more deadly than we look."

Robert was proud of her. As well as being smart and pretty, with her freckles and pale skin and strawberry blond hair, Alice was brave in front of much bigger enemies. She might not be too good at spelling or maths like he was, but she was a very clever Time Regent. He hoped she felt the same way about him. In a fleeting moment of worry, Robert wondered if she was really bluffing about their powers though. Were they really going to beat these historical giants, skilled in medieval warfare? And if he had to chose, would he, Robert, decide to stay as a Time Regent indefinitely instead of returning to the familiar life of school and family that he had in his own time?

The Sheriff's face flushed red and he shuffled uncomfortably.

"And was it you who willed us to be visible to all people out of our own time on this quest? Was that your way of fixing it unfairly to try to make sure the prophesy does not come true?" said Alice.

The Sheriff looked at her with a flicker of confusion. Robert could tell he didn't know what she was talking about. Someone else was playing tricks on them.

"Enough of prophesy! The masks will be mine. Seize them!" shouted the Sheriff.

Two men rushed towards them. Alice lifted her sword. It took her attacker by surprise. Its sharp edge cut him across his tunic. Alice started singing mysteriously. She chanted and danced around with one arm in the air. Friar Tuck looked at her then started to chant his own version alongside her. The other men stood still, suspicious of this strange girl who looked as if she was commanding something from the spirit world. Robert recognised some of the words she was using though.

"Oh, please! There is no witchcraft here, men. Only trickery," said the Sheriff. "That's a Christmas carol she is singing, not some magic chant!"

Robert looked at the Sheriff. Alice was singing the first verse of *Once in Royal David's City* to some made up, elvish tune. But how did this medieval nobleman recognise the words?

The Sheriff drew his own sword. The mighty steel blade glinted menacingly. The crossguard above the grip and pommel was covered in gold and inlaid with small jewels. There was a hole in the centre.

"That's where the seventh jewel has been kept," muttered Robert.

"Take the monk!" shouted the Sheriff. "Imprison him in my quarters."

The two men seized Friar Tuck and dragged him away.

Robert pulled an arrow from his quiver but before he could get his trembling fingers to slot it into his bow, he felt the cold metal of the Sheriff's blade on the front of his neck.

"I don't think so," sneered the Sheriff.

"Oh, I do," said a new voice behind the Sheriff. "Let him go."

The Sheriff stiffened. He still held the blade to Robert's throat.

"Sir Richard Foliot!" he breathed angrily.

"Sorry. I slipped out from your pathetic attempt to lay to siege my castle," said Sir Richard.

Over the Sheriff's shoulders, Robert saw this new

man. He was tall and strong with Saxon features. He wore armour and wielded a mighty sword. There was something about his face that resembled Sir Elias slightly.

"Your men have mostly served the forty days of their Feudal Levy," said Sir Richard. "I hear they are deserting you. Your treasure chests run dry and you cannot afford to keep making new weapons. Your trebuchet catapult is looking very wobbly, I must say. Its stone missiles are falling short of the castle walls."

"Grrrr...."

The Sheriff swung his great sword round to face Sir Richard.

"You are surrounded," said Sir Richard calmly.

All around them, Robert and Alice began to notice the trees rustle and move. Men dressed in dark red tunics decorated with branches and leaves jumped down and drew back the arrows in their flat bows.

The Sheriff's face was crimson with rage.

"I have your friend the fat monk," he sneered.

"And you will go and get him," said Sir Richard. He smiled a little too enthusiastically. "But I'll take your sword first, if you please."

The Sheriff took a step back but stopped when his back rested on the blade of a sword held by one of Sir Richard's men.

"Put it on the ground, please," said Sir Richard. "I am an honourable knight. Unlike you, I follow the chivalric code. When you return Friar Tuck I will give your sword back."

The Sheriff glanced around him and back at Sir Richard. He threw the sword onto the mossy floor and stepped closer to Sir Richard.

"You will not win this," he spat.

12

The Wellow Tunnels

Sir Richard's men stepped aside to let the Sheriff of Nottingham pass.

"Nice weapon," said Sir Richard, examining the Sheriff's sword. "Good place to hide a Time Trigger, eh?" He held its steel blade and offered the handle to Robert. "Show me what you can do."

Robert felt the heavy weight of the weapon.

"I am quite good with a modern sabre, but this is much bigger," he said.

"But I thought Little John would have shown you," said Sir Richard.

Robert remembered Little John as his teacher, Mr Reynolds, who apart from science, had taught him fencing. He had indeed spent many hours showing him and some of the other boys some tactics for older weapons and Robert had enjoyed the mock fights with the bigger swords and even once with a quarterstaff.

"So that was some kind of knights' training school?" said Robert laughing.

"You were doing the work of pages and squires I should think," said Sir Richard. He put an arm around Robert and around Alice on the other side. "Come, friends. It is good to welcome you at last, as my grandfather Elias once did. Let us away to my fireside. When you are rested, we will rescue the jolly Friar and Little John and then we shall feast and listen to the minstrels' tales and I will see how good you both are at fighting. I have heard from John that you are good shots with arrows too. We may need your skills very soon."

They walked through the trees.

"Ah, ha! Here is the place," said Sir Richard.

He bent down and brushed aside some recently disturbed leaves and soil and lifted a trap door.

"An entrance to the Wellow Tunnels. This is how we move around, in and out of the castle in secret," said Sir Richard. "Follow me!"

Robert peered after him into the damp smelling darkness. He cautiously walked down the rough stone steps, feeling the edge of each new step with his foot until his eyes adjusted in the gloom. The tunnel was very narrow, only wide enough for one person. Robert knew that this was good defence for the castle dwellers who only needed to wait and cut down one man at a time if the tunnels were ever discovered and entered by the Sheriff's men.

Alice was behind him, followed by some of Sir Richard's men. It was impossible to talk. On and on they shuffled, taking care not to injure themselves on their weapons. Water dripped on them here and there. At last Robert could see a pinhole of light ahead that grew larger with every step. Someone had opened the door ahead and was waiting for them.

They emerged into an inner chamber of the castle's keep.

"Ah, Thomas," said Sir Richard. "Thank you. I believe you have met Robert and Alice?"

The page bowed low.

"Thomas of Wellow at your service once again," said the boy.

"I think we have met your grandfather, when he was about your age, in another century?" said Alice. Robert noticed she was blushing slightly. Thomas kissed her hand and Robert felt a tiny flutter of annoyance.

"My family have served as Time Squires for many generations," said Thomas. "Your reputation has been passed on in ballads. It would be my pleasure to create any weapon or device for you that you might need my Lady. Oh, and for Robert of course."

Sir Richard's men filed past and out into the great hall. Thomas poured a sweet smelling liquor into leather goblets and passed them round.

"Herb punch to warm your blood," he said.

"Good stuff," said Robert. The honeyed mixture trickled down his throat very pleasantly.

"What shall we toast?" said Sir Richard.

"The Masks of Robin Hood," said Alice.

"Indeed," said Sir Richard, raising his goblet. "An excellent toast."

"There's a second meaning to that toast," said Alice. Her blue eyes were twinkling. "You are a kind of mask yourself. As is Sir Elias, and Little John, and anyone else down the centuries who has been guardian of the real masks. You mask the truth from the evil ones."

"That would include you and Robert too," said Sir Richard. "You are both Masks of Robin Hood in that sense."

"Rob-in-th'whode is the mask that hides all our identities, I suppose," said Alice. "And our secret mission to guard the Time Triggers."

There was a knock on the door.

Thomas opened it and spoke with the messenger. When he turned back to talk to Sir Richard, his face was white.

"It seems the Sheriff seeks to bait you, Sire," he said to Sir Richard. "He has convened an archery tournament in Nottingham at sunrise. Friar Tuck will hang unless any archer can score a perfect bull's eye."

"Will you go, Sir Richard?" said Alice.

A broad grin spread across the nobleman's sun-kissed face.

"Of course. What a pity our enemies do not show more cunning," he said. "There is no pleasure in defeating this Sheriff or any other when they cannot be more daring or original."

He looked at Robert and then at Alice.

"My dear Lady Alice," he said. "Are you ready to face this challenge?"

Robert knew she would be. Alice nodded. She was trying to look brave. She had always been a brilliant shot, even better than Robert. They always won the archery competitions at fairgrounds and on holiday.

"I'm ready too," said Robert.

"Then we are a strong team indeed," said Sir Richard. "Fetch the horses, Thomas. We will ride to the outskirts of Nottingham."

As they walked through the castle courtyard towards the drawbridge where there were horses waiting at the gatehouse, Robert remembered something.

"I've seen this Sheriff somewhere before," he said. "I can't quite remember where. And I think he has lived in our own time because he knew you were using the words of a Christmas carol in your weird chant, Alice. Nice trick by the way."

He winked at Alice. She gave him a warm grin.

"It does not surprise me," said Sir Richard as he climbed onto his horse. "The Sheriff is not a powerful Regent but he will have time travelled to spy on you. He had the seventh jewel remember. Even if he is not powerful enough to travel without Triggers or even to create a *roving* Time Tunnel

70

that would him anywhere he wanted, he could simply travel to the same spot but in another era with a Time Trigger, as we all did when we first discovered our powers."

"I remember those times when we were just beginners," said Alice.

"Things are a little more complicated, now that your strengths have developed," said Sir Richard. "But with great power comes great responsibility. You must resist the pull of the evil regents who would love you to cross over and join their greedy quests for power and domination. And you must decide whether you want to continue using your powers, for if you do, though you can do great things, your enemies will increase and you would have to leave your ordinary lives behind you."

Robert shrugged. He looked at the horse Thomas had brought for him. Alice was already on hers.

"You can ride, can't you?" said Thomas.

Robert took the reigns.

"Of course. I have had lessons."

He put his foot in the large stirrup and heaved himself up trying to look like an expert. He looked straight ahead and put his horse in a trot behind Alice and the Sheriff, hoping desperately that he could relax and not squeeze the horse's flanks too tightly if the big animal decided to go too fast.

13

Lincoln Green

It was many miles through the thick forest to Nottingham and with no paths at times, the riding was difficult. With Thomas riding behind him, Robert was determined not to fall off and he tried to ignore the various places his big saddle was rubbing.

At last Sir Richard signalled to them to slow down and be quiet. They dismounted and tied the sweaty horses to some branches where they would be hidden. The forest floor was low here. The trees ended in a wide trough in front of a high embankment with clear sky beyond. It was the edge of one safe world and up there was a dangerous new place.

They crept forwards. Robert noticed again the dark red of both Sir Richard and Thomas' tunics.

"I thought the men of Sherwood Forest wore Lincoln green clothes?" he whispered to Thomas.

"That's what this is," said Thomas looking confused.

"But it's red," said Robert.

"Lincoln green is the fine sackcloth from the white faced sheep of Lincoln," said Thomas. "It is not actually green. That pigment is too difficult to achieve. But the dark murky red we die the cloth is better for disguise all year round in the forest."

"Nobody's told them in the costume departments of the Robin Hood movies," said Robert. "The Robins charge about in bright green tights and tunics."

"Films are nothing like the truth," said Alice. "You should know that."

"Sshh!" hissed Sir Richard.

He beckoned them to crawl over to where he was spying out at the top of the rise of bracken and ferns.

When Robert peered over the crest of the mound into the world above, he saw a cleared field surrounded by colourful striped tents with flags flying. A long enclosure had been constructed in the centre with barriers for spectators and a large platform for heralds and important guests. Carpenters were erecting a temporary scaffold on one side. People were milling about everywhere. Smoke rose from the many fires.

"This is where the Sheriff holds his jousts," said Sir Richard. "And in the enclosure beyond, can you see the archery targets being set up for the dawn contest?"

Robert nodded.

"Let us make camp," said Sir Richard.

Thomas was already unravelling their makeshift beds.

"At least it is not cold," he said. "I don't think we should risk a fire."

"No. We must dine on cold venison and apples tonight, my friends," said Sir Richard. "Stay close. There may be poachers and other vagabonds at large at night."

"It looks very cosy," said Alice, helping to arrange their little camp.

The sun was setting now, sending long shadows from the edge of the mighty forest.

"Before it is quite dark, may I suggest we practice our shooting a few times?" said Sir Richard.

The others nodded. They pulled their bows and arrows from the horses' backs. Sir Richard set up a cloth target on a tree about fifty metres away.

"You will have to shoot over a greater distance tomorrow, but this will do for now," he said.

They each fired three arrows.

Sir Richard's were perfectly central every time.

"You're an amazing shot," said Robert.

"Not that much better than you," said Sir Richard. "Now let us sleep. We will need all our senses to be sharp at dawn."

Robert wrapped himself in the rough blanket and curled up head to head with Alice.

"Can you see the stars?" whispered Alice.

"Of course," said Robert. "I'll know all of them by morning. I don't think I'll be able to sleep."

"They're like a sparkling umbrella. I wonder how many there are? Maybe we should try counting them."

"Little John is somewhere out there," said Robert.

"Or maybe in another galaxy," said Alice.

"They're all joined," said Robert. "With empty black glue we call space. The gaps in between the planets and stars and galaxies, the negative bit, the real space...that's constant. It all exists at the same point in time like a gigantic lace. The gaps are joined up and touching and connected. They exist now, somewhere. You just need time to get around it. Space and time are all one really."

"Very profound," said Alice. "Anyone would think you were a Time Regent. Shut up and count stars."

"Alice... whispered Robert after a few minutes. "Are you asleep?"

"I was," Alice grunted.

"What do you think about what the others said about us having to chose whether to become great Regents?" said Robert.

Alice propped herself up on one arm.

"Does all that adventure worry you?" she said.

"Kind of," said Robert. "It's not the action or the danger though. I'm just not sure this eternal life thing is what I want. I just want to be normal."

"You're turning thoughtful all of a sudden," said Alice.

Robert could see her mischievous smile in the moonlight.

"I like my life the way it is," he said. "Don't you?"

Alice did not reply straight away. She frowned up at the night sky.

"I know what you mean," she said eventually. "But I think I can feel something bigger. We're not like the normal kids at school. We've got secrets. Big ones. And that's O.K. I'm fine with that. If I'm honest, I like it that way. Adventure is in our blood, Rob, and I'm not going to run away from what I have to do."

Robert looked at her and smiled.

"Glad you're on my side," he said.

Alice lay back down.

"Count stars!" she said.

Robert listened to Alice breathing as she fell asleep. He gently put his hand on hers and started counting the dots that sparkled in the indigo velvet of the night sky. There were so very many.

Then next thing he knew, he was being shaken by Thomas of Wellow. The sky to the East was pale now and tinged with the golden red of dawn.

"Time to wake up," said Thomas. "Put on these robes. We don't want to draw attention to ourselves yet."

Robert sat up. Alice was already changed. She had a long, brown peasant skirt over her school things and a dark shawl around her head and shoulders. Her hair twisted into two rough braids.

Robert slipped on the Lincoln green tunic.

"And these..." said Alice, smiling mischievously. "Tights!"

"I'm not wearing those!" said Robert.

"Of course you are," said Sir Richard Foliot. "With the cross garters and hide boots you will look like an ordinary page of these times."

Robert groaned but he knew Sir Richard was right. He sloped off behind a bush and changed. The tights were very thick and more like tracksuit trousers.

"De-der!" said Robert, jumping out at Alice.

"Actually, you look great," she said. "Really."

Alice smiled at him with her clear blue eyes. He hoped he wasn't blushing.

Thomas passed him a piece of stodgy bread and a goblet of weak ale. Robert was hungry and thirsty, but he still had to force himself to eat and drink this breakfast.

"Next time you're in Newark, remind me to take you for bacon and beans," he said to Thomas.

"I might hold you to that," said Thomas.

He held out his hand. After a second of hesitation, Robert took it and the two boys grinned at one another.

"Mates?" said Robert.

"Always," said Thomas, squeezing Robert's hand.

They bundled their belongings into backpacks and set off down the slope towards the archery contest. In the distance but not that far away was Nottingham Castle. It was a much larger structure than the simple keep at Wellow. It hunkered menacingly against the red dawn sky.

There were lots of people gathering now in the rainbow coloured festival. Most of them were peasants, but there were squires, knights and tradesmen and women, some from foreign shores. Sir Richard drew his cloak closer and Robert and Alice walked behind, followed by Thomas. The air was heavy with the smells of greasy cooking, animals and fires, and sweaty, unwashed bodies.

Everyone was gathering in front of the archery pit.

"Oh, no!" said Alice. She pointed to the platform with the scaffold. A cart had pulled up alongside. Friar tuck was dragged out and up the wooden steps on to the platform. Beside him was the Sheriff of Nottingham. He was dressed in fine clothes of magenta and blue velvet with gold braid. His long sleeves had ornate, castellated dags cut down the length like the top of Nottingham Castle. He wore fashionable, long toed shoes and lots of rings. Robert could see his cruel face sniggering through the loop of the hangman's noose.

14

Contest

A herald blew his horn and announced that the contest had begun.

Friar Tuck looked out across the crowd. His hands were tied but he was trying to smile.

"Is there anyone here today who would like to save the life of this traitor?" shouted the herald.

The crowd murmured but no-one came forward.

"Very well," said the Sheriff. "I know this pathetic priest is not worth wasting good arrows on. But I came here for sport. I will give a purse of silver to the winner as well."

This time several people started making their way forwards to the front. There were several squires, a peasant woman, two men from the East and one knight.

"I'm surprised there are women who know how to use bows and arrows," whispered Alice.

"Oh, yes," said Sir Richard. "The Saxon flat bow is used by everyone. Archery is encouraged for all by royal decree. The defence of the realm may depend on it. But you have long bows. They are a more recent design. They are much quicker and more powerful. An experienced long bowman can fire ten or twelve arrows in one minute and there is no defence. It will even pierce a knight's armour."

"Are we going to try, then?" said Robert.

"Not yet," said Sir Richard.

He was looking around them and across the fields towards the edge of the forest. Robert followed his gaze and understood. He recognised some faces in the crowd and in the distance he saw men emerging from the trees over the rise at the edge of the giant field, men who were dressed in Lincoln green.

The contest was underway.

The competitors took turns to fire their arrows. Gradually they were knocked out, until only one of the travellers from the East remained. The crowd cheered.

"Is this my winner then?" shouted the Sheriff. "Not one has yet scored what I consider a perfectly central bull's eye."

He was scanning the crowd.

"One of you two must go," whispered Sir Richard. "I will stay back with my men. There is no way the Sheriff will actually let Friar Tuck go. We will need to rescue him."

"I'll go," said Robert.

"Too late," said Thomas pointing.

Alice was already climbing the platform steps.

The herald bent to ask her name.

"The Lady Marion!" he shouted to the crowd.

"Well, well," said the Sheriff. "So the cowardly Foliot sends a girl to do his work does he?"

"I came alone and because I wanted to," said Alice. She buckled her leather bracers onto her wrists ready to shoot her arrows.

"Pretty girl," said the Sheriff. "You should make a pleasant hostage if you lose. Let's see if you can shoot. The rules have changed. One shot only. Begin."

The man took the first shot. It was a bull's eye. The crowd cheered. Robert could see Alice was shaking slightly. As she stepped forward, the Sheriff knocked against her, fiddling with her arrows. Robert saw the deft hand movement across Alice's back like a pick pocket.

"Oh, no!" breathed Robert. "He's bent the feathers

or something."

He pushed forward.

"Alice, stop!" he yelled.

Alice couldn't hear him. She had loaded her arrow and drew back the long flaxen bow string keeping her arm perfectly horizontal with her shoulder. The arrow shaft pressed into her cheek as she turned sideways and took aim. Robert looked around him. Sir Richard had vanished. Thomas was staring at Alice holding his breath. She was perfectly poised.

Silently, almost in slow motion, Alice released the arrow. It hit the target. The crowd gasped. Alice's peacock arrow spliced the first arrow right down the centre and sent goose feathers floating into the air. She smiled triumphantly.

"Wow! She's split the other arrow," murmured Robert.

Everyone looked at the Sheriff and waited.

"Shame," he said looking annoyed.

"Release Friar Tuck," said Alice bravely. "Oh, and by the way, I knew you were ruining my arrows. I already had one hidden up my sleeve in case you tried something. And another thing; I want my purse of silver. There are some poorer forest families who would find it very helpful."

Robert chuckled to himself.

The hangman took out his knife to cut Friar Tuck free.

"Not so fast," called the Sheriff. "This girl is the fat monk's accomplice. They are thieves and traitors. Hang them both!"

"Boo!" shouted someone in the crowd. "Unfair! She won the contest!"

Other people started to cry out.

Robert took his chance and forced his way to the base of the platform and leapt up. Thomas jumped up beside him.

"Let her go!" demanded Robert.

The Sheriff drew a broadsword from his belt.

"Take this!" shouted Thomas.

He threw Robert the jewelled sword they had taken from the Sheriff.

"That's mine!" roared the Sheriff.

"Come and get it then!" said Robert.

He stood on guard and backed along the edge of the platform.

The Sheriff lunged at him. Robert was too quick. He jumped along further and reposted, lifting the heavy weapon with all his might sending the steel blade battering across the Sheriff's chest.

The Sheriff's armour was too well made to be pierced, but the blow took his breath away. He staggered backwards.

The whole archery contest had become a huge brawl. Everyone was throwing punches at one another. Out of the corner of his eye, Robert could see Thomas fighting one of the Sheriff's men while Alice ran across to Friar Tuck. Sir Richard was waiting with a horse and cart.

Robert lifted the heavy sword again before the Sheriff had a chance to recover. He lifted it above the nobleman's head and screamed loudly. People around him stopped to watch.

"Please...no! Don't kill me..." begged the Sheriff.

"Know this, people of Nottingham," shouted Robert. "A boy and girl have beaten your cowardly Sheriff."

"Who shall we say has done this?" called someone in the crowd.

Robert glanced at Alice, then at Sir Richard.

"Tell your kinsmen that this was done by the hand of Robin Hood!" he cried.

15

A Herby Brew

Robert looked down at the snivelling Sheriff.

"I do not need to kill you," he said. "You are a laughing stock. That should be a better living punishment."

"Finish it, Robert!" called Thomas. "Or he may still be able to get the masks...."

Robert stumbled backwards. He felt dizzy and sick.

"I...I..."

He felt himself falling. The floor seemed to give way and he fell inside the earth itself.

"What's happening..."

He tried to speak. He was paralysed in complete darkness. His chest felt as if someone had tied a heavy metal band around it and they were tightening it.

He drew a mighty breath and pulled a deep, magnetic force from within his mind.

"I can feel you," he thought. "But you shall not have me. I will not lie inside one of your Time Cages in some distant galaxy. You are weak and I am strong. Remove your evil bonds from me, Prioress Gilbert of Kirklees!"

He heard a piercing shriek that echoed against every centimetre of his skull.

Once again he drew a breath against the tightening band and this time his power snapped the bonds apart. Light flooded back around him.

He was in a bumpy cart, moving fast across rough ground.

"Rob? Can you hear me?" called Alice in her soft, musical voice.

He opened his eyes.

"He's O.K!" she said.

Friar Tuck bent over him. From Robert's view lying flat on the bottom of the cart, Friar Tuck's round head looked like a planet obscuring the sun in a shiny, smiling eclipse.

"It was her..." said Robert. "The Prioress...."

"I thought as much," said Friar Tuck. "Her powers are returning. She tried to snatch you through a corridor of time down a Time Tunnel. We must return to your time to wait for the masks."

"What about Little John?" said Robert.

"I do not think we have time," said the monk. "It is the masks that matter most."

"We must try. Please," said Alice. "There must be time to try once."

"Perhaps," said Sir Richard. "Just once. It will not be pleasant."

Friar Tuck frowned.

"Can you sit up, Rob?" said Alice.

The cart slowed down.

Robert slowly dragged himself to kneeling and shuffled to the end of the cart. When it stopped, he slid off. Alice put her arm around his shoulder and helped him across the castle drawbridge. He did not try to stop her. He still felt weak and drowsy.

Inside the castle they walked back up the staircase, through a chamber and towards the doorway of the same secret cave that Robert and Alice had visited with Sir Elias Foliot a century ago.

"I'll just change out of these tights if that's O.K.?" said Robert hanging back.

Alice slipped him a grin over her shoulder.

Thomas threw the heavy oaken beam across to

bolt the door once they were all back inside.

They each sat in one of the high back chairs. Friar Tuck began to brew something in an iron pot over the flames of the fire, adding various herbs and plant leaves and other things that Robert could not quite make out.

Before long, a strong, fruity aroma filled the room. Thomas handed out goblets of the steaming brew to Robert, Alice and Sir Richard. Friar Tuck took one and sat down. Thomas stood protectively in front of the door.

"You are not drinking?" said Robert.

"He cannot," said Sir Richard. "He is a Time Squire not a Time Regent. It is us four who must drink this potion that will give us the power to reach out to John. It is a dangerous journey. If time travellers attempt it who are not ready or who do not have sufficient power, the experience could be fatal."

Robert breathed the hot steam. The vapours made his head giddy again but this time the sensation was very pleasant.

"Drink your liquor down, friends," said Friar Tuck. "Then concentrate your thoughts on the vision we have all seen of Little John in his Time Cage. Together we should be able to pull him free in a Time Tunnel and release him from his prison. I just hope we are not too late and that he is still alive."

"Are you ready Robert?" said Sir Richard.

Robert nodded.

They began to drink.

The flavours of the punch were hard to describe. One minute Robert thought they were like pineapples and peaches. But the next it was quite gritty and sour. The effect was immediate. Robert was inside the thoughts of the other three. They floated across an ocean of memories and minds, feeling things unseen and that might yet be. It was sometimes delicious. But sometimes Robert felt waves of such great fear course through him that he thought he touched the soul of every devil and evil spirit in the universe.

He reached out in his mind for Alice. He felt her near. She was frightened too. He let his thoughts entwine with hers.

Sir Richard and Friar Tuck were close by. Sir Richard's mind was strong and powerful and struck out in a path without distractions. Friar Tuck zigzagged behind. Robert's body trembled and sweat flooded through his pores.

Then suddenly they all clicked into place. They were united as they fell deeper into their own psychologies, searching for Little John across the universe.

"He's here!"

Robert felt Alice cry out. He felt a weak presence. They had found him.

Together they pulled on his faint spirit. Robert let his mind dissolve into a tunnel of power that formed from vapours into a mighty hollow trunk of light. Still they pulled. Robert thought that now, just when they needed him most, his strength might go.

He cried out.

His eyes opened. Thomas was wiping Sir Richard's brow with a wet cloth. Alice lay slumped into her chair. Friar Tuck was muttering with his eyes still closed.

"Alice...."

Robert tried to get up but his knees buckled. Thomas looked across at Alice.

"She's only sleeping," he said.

Robert frowned. He forced himself to stand up and stepped over to her chair, supporting himself on the high back. He felt for the pulse on her wrist.

"She's alive!" he said. He sat her up and placed a flannel on her forehead. Her eyes flickered and slowly opened as she took an enormous breath.

"She will be fine," said Sir Richard. "She is very strong."

The sensation and power in Robert's body was coming back. Pins and needles flickered in and out of every muscle.

"But where is John?" he said.

Thomas pointed towards the fire. A man lay unconscious on the hearth rug, shivering and calling out.

"He came back in your mighty Time Tunnel some time ago," said Thomas. "I have attended to him. I have placed a poultice on his wounds and fed him herbs and water. I think he will live. When the friar is recovered he will know what to do. You four have been unconscious for quite some time with the effort of your actions but you have rescued Little John, the chief guardian of the masks."

Robert staggered across to the man by the fire. He could see his black beard now. On the fur below, his face flickering in the fire light, was his science teacher Mr Reynolds.

16

Green Men and Minstrels

Robert knelt down.

"Mr Reynolds, Sir, can you hear me?" whispered Robert gently.

The man's eyes slowly flicked open.

"Sorry..." he mumbled.

Robert was surprised. It felt odd having a teacher apologise to him.

"Why are you sorry, Sir?" said Robert.

"I failed you..." said the big man.

He propped himself up. Thomas had bandaged the deepest wounds on his chest and leg but Robert winced at the number of other cuts across the man's body. The Prioress had been vicious. She had stabbed him many times.

"Robert, you must stop calling me Sir from now on. My name is John. It is I who should address you as Sire, for I am your servant," said Little John. "And I failed to protect you. Someone even managed to place a curse upon you that makes you visible out of your own time and much more vulnerable than usual. That you are still alive is a credit to your own powers."

He looked down miserably, clutching his painful leg.

"We are safe," said Robert.

"But I should have been more careful. The Prioress is a deadly foe," said Little John. "You and Alice have proved the ballads right though. You outwitted her anyway. Perhaps my time as guardian is drawing to a close now that you two are here. You will be the heirs to the Foliot dynasty. You are the next guardians of the masks."

He smiled over Robert's shoulder. Alice had come over.

"Don't die on us yet, Sir," she said. "I think we'd both be grateful of your protection. It was not your fault that we were brought into this before you had prepared us."

"My Lady," said Little John. "Please call me John. And I must disagree. I shall bear the guilt of my stupidity forever. I cannot believe I did not see Miss Gilbert for who she really is. It was she who gave you the Time Trigger and created the Time Tunnel to Sherwood Forest into the grip of the Sheriff. She must have sensed I was about to tell you and decided to kill you before you could fulfil your destiny and find the masks. She kept me as a hostage as insurance but she would not have cared if I had died."

"She will be growing strong again," said Sir Richard. He helped himself to a drink and warmed his hands against the flames of the fire. "Robert and Alice must go back to their time and reach the masks before she does."

"But we don't know where they are," said Alice.

"I had almost worked it out," said Little John. "I have made notes and calculations for as long as I have been the guardian these few hundred years. I had charts, but I fear the Prioress has them now. Oh, how could I have been so stupid...!"

He fell back in despair.

"Come, John," said Friar Tuck. He bent over to check his bandages. "We all make mistakes. We will work something out. Pass me more spider silk, Thomas, please. This wound is leaking still. And more yarrow. Thank goodness I picked extra when I saw it growing in the forest last week. It will slow the bleeding and ease the pain."

Robert suddenly remembered something.

"Your charts! Of course. Is this what you mean?" he said.

From inside his filthy blazer, he pulled out the scroll he had taken from the teacher's desk drawer when he and Alice had found the empty, blood stained office.

Little John sat up.

"Holy Mary! Yes. This is wonderful!" he said.

Robert passed him the scroll.

"What does it all mean?" said Alice.

"These are my coded notes," said Little John. He wrenched himself to standing. He was almost smiling now. He took the scroll across to the oak table. "It is one of three charts. But it is the most important one. Well done! We can use a lot from this. But she will have the rest. If the Prioress can break my codes, we may have unpleasant company on our quest."

Little John began to check the markings on the scroll.

"Friend," said Sir Richard. "What must we do?"

"I need some time to translate and to write it out," said Little John. "You can all go and eat while I work. I will only need a few hours."

"Here is a quill. And more parchment," said Thomas. "Shall I open the door, Sire?"

Sir Richard nodded.

"I hope the cooks have something ready in the castle kitchens. I have a fancy for a small feast. We have much to celebrate, my friends," he said.

"I will prepare the hall, Sire," said Thomas.

"Do you need any help, John?" said Alice. She was watching Little John as he leant over the manuscript, examining it intently. "The markings are beautiful. What do they mean?"

"Only I can do this, my child," said Little John. "The drawings represent clues I have gathered about the masks. The moons tell me about the dates and the trees are arranged in coded maps. On my journeys across England and Europe and even to the East, I have heard tales and collected clues. The coded ballads and poems tell of what has been and the Shell of Destiny has interpreted much of what is to come." He looked into Alice's eyes. "And always they mention you and Robert. Most of what is written here is about you. Robin Hood and the Lady Marion will be reborn. The Green Man and the Green Lady of Sherwood will lay claim to the power of the masks."

"I have heard of the Green Man," said Alice. "Isn't it that bearded face with leaves around it that you find on churches and houses?"

"Yes. It is an ancient symbol stretching back many thousands of years that symbolises rebirth and renewal," said Little John. "I have found so many references to the young Green Man and Green Lady, youngsters of Sherwood Forest of your time who are the rebirth of a legend, the legend of Robin Hood. And some clues gave your ancestry. Your mother's maiden name was Hastings, wasn't it Robert? She is a direct descendent of the Foliots. And Alice is descended also, from Margaret Foliot who lived in Wellow Castle before she disappeared. She was a Time Regent. Some say she was the best Rob-in-th'whode. By piecing together all the clues I was able to find you. It was then my job to watch over you and prepare you for your destiny."

"Does that mean we are related?" said Robert looking at Alice.

She screwed her nose up at him playfully.

"Not really. Over the centuries the families have diverged," said Little John.

"We might be hundredth cousins, twenty times removed or something," laughed Alice.

"Some call the Green Man symbol the 'foliate man' because of the foliage or leaves coming out of his ears and mouth," said Sir Richard. "Does it remind you of anything?"

"Your surname?" said Robert.

"Partly. It is true that Foliot is derived from the French *feuille verte* meaning green leaf," said Sir Richard.

"And it looks like your men!" said Alice. "With their camouflage leaves."

"Exactly. Another veiled clue for those who have the knowledge. But it is all just camouflage for the real secret: the powerful masks," said Sir Richard.

Thomas returned.

"The feast is ready, Sire," he said.

"Let us eat until John is ready," said Sir Richard.

Robert and Alice followed the others down the stairway and into the central hall. Wonderful smells of roasting meat and vegetables wafted towards them. They sat down in the ornately crafted chairs. Servants ushered in with platters of food.

"Not quite like pizzas, eh?" said Alice, helping herself to berries.

"Better!" said Robert, tucking in with his fingers. "What meat is this?"

"Partridge," said Friar Tuck. "My favourite."

Robert hesitated. "Good though," he said, taking a second helping. "Much healthier than all our modern chemicals and stuff, I bet."

"I prefer red deer venison," said Sir Richard. "Thomas, have we no minstrels?"

He waved towards the polished wooden minstrel gallery above.

"I recommend the ginger and honey cakes," said Friar Tuck. "Although personally, I am developing a taste for your sugared dough-nuts, Alice. Perhaps when you return, you could bring me a bag?"

Alice grinned at the fat monk.

"It would be my pleasure," she said, wiping grease from her chin and swigging the mead.

Robert poured himself a second cup of drink. The sweet liquor felt good. Robert was tired. He let his head fall back and listened as a young singer stood on the balcony and began to strum on his instrument, singing a rhythmic chant of poetry. His rich voice mixed in Robert's head with the laughter of friends and the crackle of the fire and the clank of plates and glasses.

The minstrel sang a ballad that talked of a good knight who owed a debt to an evil abbot. The knight was helped by the heroes of the forest under the command of Rob-in-th'whode. The heroes defeated the cruel Sheriff of Nottingham who had tried to lay siege to their castle in the forest.

Robert opened his eyes. There was a disturbance.

"I have finished," said Little John, bursting in. "I have written down all the clues. I now need Alice and Robert to make sense of them so we can find out exactly where the masks are buried. I only hope we are in time and that the Prioress has not got there first."

17

Poetry

Everyone looked at the drawings.

Robert frowned. Nothing made sense.

"That is a gate," said Alice. "But who is the man?"

"Some kind of sentry," said Little John. "He wears a helmet."

"Is he a Norman soldier?" said Friar Tuck.

"No. He is of the twenty-first century. He always talks in numbers."

"Strange," said Alice.

"And what is this funny, lumpy wall thing in the centre?" said Robert.

"I had hoped you might know it's meaning," said Little John looking disappointed. "Its image recurs in the visions of the Shell of Destiny along side the mechanical digger machine that looks like a metal trebuchet."

"The JCB," said Alice.

"And what is this poetry?" said Robert.

"This has been passed on by minstrels throughout Sherwood Forest for many years," said Little John. "Sir Richard will recognise it, just as his grandfather, Sir Elias would have done."

"We have stopped them singing it since my grandfather and John realised its meaning, in case the Sheriff should work it out," said Sir Richard.

"Yes. I wrote it down in code to keep it secret from prying eyes," said Little John. "I think Alice should read it to us, since she is mentioned in the first verse."

Alice read aloud.

*"Ever we wait young Lady M,
'Tis thee who has the task.
She and her shadow look on high
And hide the sacred masks.*

*In Lincoln green and Lincoln's tower
Search on and be ahead.
Buried treasure, power and great wealth.
Dig deep the box, 'tis said.*

*To Robin Hood and Lady M
Our freedom, sirs, entrust.
If guardians fall to evil foe
Flee Sherwood then ye must.*

*When carts can fly and boxes talk
Descendents come at last.
The Wellow secret will be dug
When future meets the past."*

"What does it all mean?" said Robert.

"I know that the flying carts and talking boxes refer to your modern age with aeroplanes and mobile phones," said Little John. "That helped me to find you. And that the masks will be dug up in Sherwood Forest near to Wellow in your time. The possible references to Lincoln and Lady M's shadow I have not yet fathomed."

"Well, if we are rested, I think we need to go and search in your modern time," said Little John. "There is not a moment to lose."

"I need to stay here and distract our friend the Sheriff," said Sir Richard. "You should accompany Robert and Alice, John. That is how it is meant to be."

"Will we see you again?" said Robert.

"Oh, I think so," said Sir Richard. "Take your weapons though. You will be able to come here to the safety of my castle if you are trapped by danger that you cannot evade otherwise."

"That sounds reassuring," said Alice.

"And don't forget my dough-nuts!" shouted Friar Tuck.

Robert and Alice gathered their things and stood with Little John. He looked well again. The fat monk's medicines were very good.

Robert took out the jewel Time Trigger and they held hands.

"Stand back, friends," said Sir Richard. "These Regents will create a mighty Time Tunnel."

Robert closed his eyes and joined his thoughts with Alice and Little John. He felt comfortable next to Alice. Perhaps it was their shared ancestry. If he was to become a powerful Time Regent he would like it if Alice was there too.

The Time Tunnel grew around them into a mighty spiral of white light. If it burnt a circle on the ground, it did not harm the travellers inside. The journey flashed on, cutting through space and time in a brilliant stellar pathway at immeasurable speeds. Robert felt the pulsing thrill of time travel that was his secret gift. Centuries shrank to minutes.

The impact of the journey's end threw them onto their knees. Robert caught Alice as she fell towards him. Her hair smelt of peat fires. She smiled up at him with her clear blue eyes. He felt a pang of loss, as if someone he knew was going to die. He held her tighter.

"Thanks," she said. "I'm O.K. now."

"Do you feel the danger?" said Robert quietly.

Alice stared at him. She shivered.

"Yes, I do. It must be very great for you to sense it before me," she said.

"I think someone is going to die," said Robert. "We're not all going to make it through this quest are we?"

They were in a field on the outskirts of Wellow. People milled about on the village green, around young girls dressed in white, twisting the long ribbons around the famous maypole. It was the village fete. Morris dancers jingled and clapped.

"I've felt that smell of death already," said Alice.

Little John called them across.

"We need a car. I have one parked down the little lane opposite. I have kept it here for use in emergencies. Follow me."

They walked away from the main Newark road and down a farm track. About a hundred metres on, Little John started to pull aside some branches.

"A Mini!" said Alice. "My favourite car. I want one of these when I can drive."

"It's a little car for a big man," said Robert.

"Um, I know," said Little John grinning. "I needed it to be small but fast. This engine is fantastic. It's not that small inside either."

Alice climbed into the back seat and Robert strapped himself in the front. Little John, looking slightly squashed in the driver's seat, started the engine. It was deep and powerful.

"Wow! That's not a normal Mini engine," said Robert.

John grinned mischievously and swung the car around doing a tidy U-turn on the track. The Mini's oversized tyres gripped the dirt beautifully.

"Where are we going?" said Robert.

"To my house. I had to find somewhere hidden. I rented a barn on the road to Nottingham."

They drove off.

"Stop!" shouted Robert.

Little John slammed on the brakes.

"I thought I saw the Sheriff," said Robert. "Up there on that platform where they're giving out prizes at that fair."

Little John and Alice stood out of the car. John brought out some little binoculars from the glove compartment. They scanned the crowd. Some officials were presenting prizes.

"I can't see anyone that looks like him," said Little John.

Robert borrowed the binoculars.

"Funny," he said. "I could have sworn...."

"You're spooked!" said Alice.

Robert made a face at her. He really thought he had seen a face that looked like the Sheriff, but he had to agree there was no-one there like that now.

They got back into the car and drove past the entrance to the Center Parcs holiday park where Robert had spent two short holidays with Alice and her family. He liked it, especially the archery and quad bikes and the high wires.

"We had some good times in there, didn't we?" said Alice. "Remember the climbing wall? You only just beat me to the top."

Robert turned and grinned at Alice.

Then he frowned.

Alice looked at him strangely too.

"That's it. The knobbly wall on John's charts!" said Robert.

Alice nodded enthusiastically.

"I think we've found it," she said. "It's the climbing wall at Center Parcs."

18

Road Rage

Little John stopped the Mini again. He turned around and sped off in the direction of the holiday park.

"That's why you had to be here. Only you could recognise the clues," he said. "Mind you, a climbing wall seems a little unnecessary when there are all these trees! Let's go in, shall we?"

"We can't," said Alice.

She looked at Robert.

"The guard!" they both said together.

"I bet that's the sentry man you described," said Robert.

"Why would he speak in numbers?" said Little John. "I've been trying to work that one out, but even all the scientific knowledge I have gained over my years has not revealed the answer to me."

"I think I might know," said Alice.

"Go on," said Little John. "There are things only you two time travellers can bring to this quest. Tell me, Alice."

"When we arrived, we had to give a code to the gateman to be let in. Somehow we have to get a code," she said.

"Hmm. I suppose we could go home and make a booking," said Robert.

"But what is to stop us time travelling there using a Time Tunnel?" said Alice.

"Then why would the numbers mean anything?" said Little John.

"They don't!" said Alice. "They're just a clue to

make us find this place. That's all. We could go through the gate like normal people if we got ourselves booked in but that will take time. We're not normal though, are we? We can time travel."

Something suddenly bumped into the back of the car. They were thrown forwards. The whiplash movement sent a sharp pain down Robert's neck.

"Someone's ramming us!" said Little John. "Get out, quickly!"

Robert opened the door and leapt out, dragging his long bow after him. John was already out of the driver's side.

A four-wheel drive vehicle with blacked out windows was about to smash into the little Mini again.

"Alice!" cried Robert.

But before he could lift the front seat forwards to let Alice out, the heavy truck crunched into the Mini sending it spinning towards the ditch where it tipped onto its front and smashed into a tree.

Robert could see Alice was injured. She wasn't moving and blood was seeping down the side of her head. The driver of the truck revved the engine. The truck lurched forwards towards Robert.

Suddenly, he felt himself falling. Little John had pushed him and he tumbled into the ditch.

At the same time, he heard Little John's scream.

Robert dragged himself up. Little John lay very still, in front of the truck. The driver was trying to reverse but the vehicle's wheels were stuck in the mud on the edge of the ditch. Another car approached from the other direction.

Robert thought he heard the driver in the truck swearing. The other car slowed down and stopped. A lady got out.

"I've just dialled for an ambulance on my mobile phone!" she shouted, rushing towards them.

"No! Stay where you are!" shouted Robert, trying to warn the lady.

She didn't hear him.

On the other side of the black-windowed truck, Robert heard the driver's door open. A hooded figure got out.

"Oh, hello," said the lady, recognising the driver.

"Go back!" shouted Robert to the lady again.

It was too late. Robert heard the faint hissing sound of an arrow being released. It landed in the woman's leg. She fell to the floor screaming. The hooded figure ran towards her car and drove off.

For a moment, Robert stood still. His head was swimming. Little John lay on one side of him and the injured lady on the other. In front of him, in the Mini, was Alice.

His head cleared and he ran over to Alice. The Mini's engine was still running and he could smell petrol.

Robert pushed the front seat forwards with all his might and tugged on Alice. She was wedged. One of her legs was stuck under the front passenger seat. He pulled again. Somewhere in the distance he could hear sirens.

"COME...ON!" he grunted, heaving her lifeless body towards him.

Alice started to wake up.

She shook her head.

"Alice, help me here!" said Robert. "I think this car is about to blow up!"

Alice squinted at him. With his arms under her shoulders, he lifted her body. She freed her legs and Robert pulled her through the gap behind the seat. They fell onto the ground and Robert rolled the two of them further down the ditch.

The car exploded.

A pulse of pain thundered through Robert's ears.

An orange flash ballooned upwards and engulfed the Mini in a ball of flame. Thick black smoke billowed up into the sky. Robert covered Alice with his body. He felt the heat of the explosion on his back, singing his blazer. A few metres away, Little John still lay on the road under the front wheels of the truck.

"If guardians fall to evil foe..." echoed in Robert's mind.

19

Death of a Hero

The sirens were very close now. Robert rested Alice on the ground. She was looking a better colour now. He gave her his handkerchief to press against the cut on her head.

"Who was it?" said Alice.

"I didn't see," said Robert. "But that poor lady knew who it was."

An ambulance pulled up, followed by a fire engine. Then Robert heard the sound of another engine approaching quietly from the other direction. He felt a dark shadow cross his soul. He sensed treachery again.

"It's that lady's car again!" said Robert. "Whoever it was has turned round to finish us off. They know they've been recognised."

He ducked down. The ambulance crew were attending to the injured lady and Little John. The firemen were trying to put out the blaze. No-one spotted Alice and Robert in the ditch.

Robert squinted through the smoke. Someone was walking towards the scene on the other side.

"Oh, no!" he whispered. "Now we're in trouble. Look Alice. Tell me I'm not imagining it again this time, please. It really is him."

Alice rubbed her head and crawled alongside Robert.

"You're not imagining it," said Alice. "That's him. That's the Sheriff of Nottingham's evil face. But now he's wearing a posh suit. Who is he trying to be?"

"Sshh! Listen," said Robert.

"Officer! Good Lord!" said the Sheriff. "Whatever has happened here? That woman has crashed her truck into the Mini has she?"

He was looking at the lady. She was unconscious with an oxygen mask over her face. She was being lifted onto a stretcher.

"Will she make it?" said the Sheriff.

"It looks bad, I'm afraid," said one of the paramedics. "She's lost a lot of blood."

The Sheriff smiled.

"And that poor fellow over there?" said the Sheriff in his clipped, upper class tones.

"He's dead I'm afraid," said a fireman.

Alice gasped and sank down.

"Little John is dead," she muttered.

Robert was still watching.

"The Sheriff's looking around for us, Alice," he said. "He's coming this way. We're going to have to get out of here. We'll use the Time Trigger."

Alice looked at Robert. Tears were running down her cheeks.

"But Little John...we can't leave him," she breathed.

"We've got too," said Robert. He took her arm and squeezed the Time Trigger jewel. Foot steps were approaching along the road. "It's what he would have wanted. We're the guardians of the masks now." He wiped Alice's tears away. "Think of Center Parcs. Visualise the climbing wall. The masks must be there. Now!"

Robert hurled his thoughts towards travelling through time. The Time Tunnel was bumpy. Someone else was trying to stop it. The forces of another power intruded.

The tunnel held. Robert and Alice parried the

outsider and deflected him. This tunnel felt hotter than usual. Robert's face smarted, like when he'd been out in the summer sun all day without any sun cream to protect him.

They landed with a thud. The knees of Robert's school trousers ripped as he was dragged to the floor in the rough landing.

"Could have done with a parachute that time," he moaned.

"It's worked!" said Alice. "We have to get up though. Now! Someone else is not far behind us, I can feel them."

It was dark. They had arrived at night. The familiar structures of the adventure equipment in the holiday park skulked like dinosaur silhouettes in the trees against the crisp light of the full moon.

"Over here," said Robert. "Let's get our breath back for a minute on this veranda. It's a staff hut or something. How's your head?"

"It aches, but I'm O.K," said Alice. "Thanks for pulling me out back there."

She offered him a high five.

"Any time," said Robert. He was about to play silly and make James Bond noises but he decided not to. This wasn't a time for messing around. Once he might have done, but on this occasion he stopped himself.

"Let's go," he said. "The climbing wall is this way."

He tried to shake the picture of Little John on the ground from his head. Robert felt different somehow. He knew he did. Something had changed in him. He felt harder and tougher and older.

Alice was walking on, her feet silent on the forest floor. They could see the glimmer of the tourist lodges flickering like fairy lights through the trees and reflecting on the still surface of the lake. In the distance they heard the scattered laughter of groups of late night party goers enjoying their holiday, oblivious to the perilous quest being played out in the darkness of the trees.

"I know where I've seen the Sheriff before," said Robert suddenly. "I've just recognised him. He's a politician. I've seen him on the local television news. He got elected when the last guy died mysteriously a few months ago."

"That makes sense," said Alice. "Like Sir Richard Foliot said, the enemies of Robin Hood will camouflage themselves in high office so they can use all their sneaky powers."

"What do you think he will do if he gets to these masks first?" said Robert.

"He's a politician. If these masks are the powerful Time Triggers everyone seems to think they are, he could use their power to win wars and control energy supplies. He could travel back and forwards in time and influence everything. He could take over this country and others I should think," said Alice.

"Scary stuff," said Robert.

"What are we going to do with the masks, then?" asked Alice.

She was almost smiling.

"Bury them again?" said Robert. "On the other hand...."

He gave a silly, evil laugh. Alice thumped him.

"It's here," she said, pointing to the tall shape that loomed out of the adventure park.

Climbing ropes were tied up around it like giant nooses.

"So where are these masks then?" said Robert.

"That looks interesting," said Alice. "They're doing some sort of construction work here. They're making a new activity area up in the trees. Looks good!"

"And there's another clue," said Robert.

He nodded towards the tractors and JCBs fenced off a few metres away.

Suddenly, he froze. He signalled to Alice to get down. He had heard a twig snapping in the forest behind them.

"We're not alone, are we?" whispered Alice.

Robert shook his head. Somewhere out there in the blackness, someone else was creeping about in Sherwood Forest.

20

Metal Detector

They heard another stick break.

"Whoever it is, they're not one of Sir Richard Foliot's men, that's for sure," whispered Robert. "You wouldn't be able to hear them approaching unless they wanted you to."

They lay face down and very still. Robert could hear his pulse thumping very fast in his ears. A shadowy figure passed by just to their left and climbed over the fencing wire surrounding the building works.

Alice and Robert lifted their heads and looked into the darkness.

"They're poking about looking for something," said Alice quietly.

The shadow stopped and crouched down to scrape at the ground.

"Something's buried there," said Robert. He looked at Alice. "Do you think they've found the masks?"

Alice shook her head.

There was a clicking sound.

"Listen. I recognise that sound," said Alice. Something started humming at a low pitch. "It's a metal detector."

"That silhouette is too small to be the Sheriff," said Robert. "I reckon it's the Prioress."

"What do we do?" said Alice. "She obviously thinks the masks are buried somewhere here. What if she finds them?"

Just then the noise of the metal detector switched to a high pitched alarm.

"She's found something!" said Robert.

The figure started digging. They heard a muffled curse. Robert let his breath go.

"Phew! They don't sound pleased. It's probably someone's key," said Alice.

The alarm noise on the metal detector sounded again.

This time the shadow stayed kneeling, digging with a small spade. Whoever it was stopped and started brushing the dirt from something.

"Oh, no!" said Alice. "She seems too interested in whatever she has found."

"Should we attack? There are two of us," said Robert. His grip tightened on his bow.

"Not yet," said Alice. "It might be another false alarm."

The person started digging frantically and tugged on whatever was buried. Suddenly, the shadow fell backwards with the force of pulling, as the object came free.

"Now!" shouted Robert.

He leapt forward. Alice followed.

The surprise was enough. They bowled the shadow over just as the person was about to stand up.

Alice sat on her struggling hostage and pulled back the cowled hood.

"I was right!" she said. "The Prioress of Kirklees. Please don't tell me you're doing God's work trespassing and digging up forests in the middle of the night. You're poaching. I'm sure there must be a nasty punishment for that in your time, eh? Shall we chop off your hands or put you in the stocks for all to see?"

The Prioress' face curled into an evil snarl.

"I suppose you're the one who willed us to be visible?" said Robert.

"Bah! Novice stuff!" spat the Prioress.

"Well actually it's been much better being seen," said Alice. "We feel much more at home and we can call upon more help from the men and women of the forest if we need them."

The Prioress curled her lips and went red with anger.

"Your arrogant cheek will not save you!" she shouted.

Robert smiled when she bit her own lip in her fury.

"And what have we here?" he said. "What is the little box your boney hands are clutching, madam? I think I'll take that...."

The Prioress struggled but Alice had her thin frame pinned securely to the ground under her.

"Give it back to me!" shouted the Prioress. "It's mine!"

"Mine! Mine! Mine!" teased Robert. "Tut, tut! No manners. Didn't your mother ever tell you that 'mine' was a rude thing to say?"

Robert examined the ancient box. He brushed the last bits of mud from its hinges. It looked as if it was made of very tarnished silver.

"I could do with a hand here," said Alice. The prioress was wriggling and had got one arm free. She pulled at Alice's hair and screamed.

Robert knelt down and held a sharpened arrow tip to the Prioress' throat.

"Ha! You'll never use it!" cackled the woman.

"Oh, I wouldn't bet on that," said Robert. "We children are all grown up now. You can kill and so can we."

Alice looked at Robert with one eyebrow lifted. He winked at her.

"I think it's our turn to take a hostage," he said.

He put the box down and reached towards some workman's rope that lay beside the fencing. Alice lifted the woman's hands and Robert wound the rope around her wrists several times before tying it securely.

"Stand up!" shouted Robert.

Alice pulled the woman to her feet and Robert looped another piece of rope between her tied hands to pull her along with. He tossed Alice the box.

"Back to the staff hut," he said to Alice, pulling the struggling Prioress behind him.

Alice nodded and ran ahead. When she got to the hut she used a rock to shatter a small pane of glass above the door handle. She reached in carefully and released the lock. They went inside. Robert kicked the door closed behind them. He pushed the Prioress onto a chair in front of the racks of climbing harnesses and other equipment.

"You won't succeed," she said. "You are too weak to command the forces of time locked in that box. The masks are mine...."

"Oh, shut up," said Robert as he slipped his tie off and wound it around her mouth to gag her. "Now what have we here?"

The box was locked but Robert could feel the clasp had softened over the centuries. He started to prise it open with an arrowhead. The metal snapped.

Alice looked inside with him. To Robert's surprise, there were no little masks inside, just a leather roll. He unravelled it.

Inside the leather was a piece of parchment fastened with a silver ring. He gently took it out. The Prioress was quiet now, watching intently.

Robert and Alice looked at the parchment, then at each other. Alice held her finger to her lips.

"Sshh! What's in here stays our secret," she said.

21

Brains and Beauty

It had started to rain outside the cabin. The gentle patter quickly changed into hammering sheets, battering the small wood structure. A single flash of lightening cracked to the ground nearby. Only seconds later came the thunder. The almighty boom sent shock waves through the cabin and roared through Robert's ears. The eye of the storm was right above them.

Robert snapped the lid of the box closed and looked around him. The Prioress had vanished.

"Where is she?" he screamed, turning desperately around, scanning the darkness.

The next flash of lightening cut through the night and he saw her. Somehow she had slipped her bonds. She was standing with her back to one corner of the cabin wielding a climbing axe.

She threw it at Robert. But he was quicker. He ducked deftly to one side and lunged towards the woman. She reached beside her and held out a stake. Just in time, Robert stopped. The point of the stake brushed his shirt but did not pierce his flesh. He stepped back. The prioress followed, matching each of his strides until he felt his back thud against the far wall of the cabin.

"Give me the box!" said the Prioress quietly. "Or I will carve out your entrails and send them back to Sir Richard in it!"

Out of the corner of his eye, Robert could see Alice moving silently towards the Prioress' back. He kept his stare firmly on the Prioress.

111

"What is in here is no use to you without me," said Robert. "The ballads have always told that the young Robin Hood and Lady Marion of this century would find the masks, and so we must. If I die, you will never see the Masks of Robin Hood."

He could feel the Prioress hesitate. In that moment, Alice attacked. She took the last step to the Prioress and slipped a rope over her head and around her throat.

The Prioress dropped the stake and gasped for breath. Alice tightened the rope. Robert lunged for the door and flung it open. Lightening struck a tree nearby, illuminating the whole adventure playground in a fleeting wave of brilliance.

"Let's go, Alice!" shouted Robert, almost drowned out by the clap of thunder.

For a moment, he wondered if Alice was going to let go of the rope at all. When she did, she pushed the wheezing Prioress to the ground and leapt out after Robert into the driving rain.

They ran and ran, dodging trees and gateways and sliding and slipping in the torrents of water that gushed down the forest paths, turning them into brooks and bogs.

They crossed the end of the lake over the rope bridge. Robert slipped. He slid towards the side of the bridge towards the water. His longbow, strung out across his back, caught on the side rope. He felt Alice's hand grabbing the collar of his blazer and he hauled himself backwards onto his side.

"Cheers," he managed to say, with rain running down his face and plastering his hair against his head. Alice helped him up.

"We can't have you doing all the heroics now, can we?" said Alice grinning.

"We have to keep moving," panted Robert. "If we

get to the swimming dome there will be some people. We should be a bit safer there. Even if she makes herself invisible to the people of our time, she would have more difficulty attacking us there."

"Look after that bow," said Alice. "It's the only weapon we've got since I lost mine in the car crash."

"You seemed pretty competent with a rope," said Robert. "Almost as good as with a bow and arrow. I'll bear that in mind if I annoy you too much. You're a dangerous woman."

Alice pretended to look surprised.

"Maid Marian is not just a pretty face," she said sarcastically.

"Um. Brains and beauty are a deadly combination, I can see," boomed a man's voice behind them at the end of the rope bridge.

Robert and Alice swung round.

"The Sheriff!" muttered Alice.

"We do communicate you know," said the Sheriff. "Just because we started our careers in the thirteenth century doesn't mean the Prioress and I have not familiarised ourselves with your modern technology like mobile phones. We wouldn't be very clever Time Regents if we couldn't do that."

He smiled cruelly.

"I see you've also developed a liking for modern tooth whitening techniques," said Robert.

"One does like to look one's very best," the Sheriff sneered sarcastically. "I have really enjoyed my visit, blending in with the people of your time. I plan to extend my stay and try out lots more of your modern discoveries, once I have the masks. Now be a good boy, Robert, and hand over the box."

Robert and Alice turned and ran towards the lights of the tropical dome. The Sheriff ran after them. They were almost at the door when it swung open and a team of armed police men and women fanned out in front of them in a line.

"Oh, thank God!" said Alice. "We need the police. This man is chasing us and...."

To Robert and Alice's amazement, the policemen lifted their rifles towards them. Someone switched on a floodlight.

"Stay where you are!" called the officer in charge through a megaphone. "We have you surrounded."

"But..." Alice looked at Robert in shock.

"Thank you officer," said the Sheriff of Nottingham, as he swaggered towards them. "These are the ones. They are deadly. They have already caused two deaths on the road and have tried to kill a woman teacher who was tracking them."

"It's O.K, Sir," said the chief policeman. "Stay back please. We will take it from now. You can go back to your important political meeting with the government ministers. Thank you for taking the time to inform us."

"My pleasure, officers," said the Sheriff with a grotesque smile. "There is one small thing. These two have stolen something that belongs to me...."

"Hold my hand," whispered Robert to Alice.

He reached into his blazer pocket.

The policemen cocked their rifles ready to fire.

"It's here...your item," called Robert.

The Sheriff moved towards them, his greedy eyes narrowing in pleasure.

Robert closed his eyes and squeezed Alice's hand. He felt a surge of power as he summoned all his time travelling powers. He sensed Alice doing the same.

"Fire, you idiots!" shouted the Sheriff. "Shoot them now, before they escape..."

22

Invisible Clue

Through squinting eyes, Robert saw the policemen shade themselves from the heat that was the Time Tunnel. The vortex sped them on. Robert couldn't hear the Sheriff's angry voice any more. They were somewhere else.

"Thank goodness," said Alice.

They were back in the great hall of Sir Richard Foliot's castle.

Thomas of Wellow rushed to help them, calling for his master.

"We're fine, really," said Robert.

"You look wet," said the merry voice of Friar Tuck. "But you are well, I think?"

"But where is John?" said Sir Richard Foliot, running into the hall.

Alice and Robert looked at each other and back at Sir Richard.

"He, er..." Robert stammered. He couldn't think what words to use.

"He's dead, isn't he?" said Sir Richard.

Robert nodded slowly.

"My God! This time we have met the most deadly of enemies," said Sir Richard. He turned away sadly and slumped into a chair. "What happened? I tried to watch you in the Shell of Destiny, but for once its vision was too cloudy, almost as if someone here was blocking it to prevent me seeing. Perhaps I could have travelled one last time..."

Alice carefully told their story.

"The stuff of legends indeed," said Friar Tuck. "I

115

think our minstrels will have much to say about this tale of bravery and loss. But you have the silver box still, do you not?"

Robert put it on the table and opened it.

"My ancestors were very clever, it seems," said Sir Richard. "They did not bury the actual masks but a clue instead. What is written on the parchment, friends?"

Robert unravelled the small scroll.

Everyone gasped.

"Nothing?" boomed Sir Richard. "You mean my greatest friend and the chief guardian of the masks gave his life for nothing?"

"May I see?" said Friar Tuck.

He lifted the parchment up against the light of a candle.

"Take care. . " said Robert, taking a step closer.

"I will not burn it," said the monk. "Ah, ha! It is as I thought. There are words here, written invisibly with juices that show up in direct light."

Robert and Alice bent to look.

"What does it say?" said Sir Richard.

Friar tuck squinted at the blurred, translucent streaks. He wiped his sweaty brow. Robert caught the strange expression on the monk's face. He cast a furtive glance at Alice and a fearful look behind him but smiled quickly when he saw that Robert was watching him.

Friar Tuck started to read.

As Lady M, my duty lies
the masks to move and hide.
So like my green man, thou art me.
My poetry confide.

Tall tower and pole, my friends ye seek
The view from jousting green.
The secret of the masks is blind
But not to our May Queen.

"It's signed '*M*', isn't it?" said Robert. "M for Marion, I suppose."

"I think it means another Maid Marion moved the masks and wrote the poetry of clues that became a ballad," said Alice. "Don't you remember how Sir Elias Foliot thought he saw a woman's shadow across the visions of the Shell of Destiny? I bet it was this other Marion, not the Prioress. How exciting! Another Marion in another age, fighting to keep the masks a secret from our enemies."

"I think you are right," said Sir Richard. "You, Alice, are the last legend of Marion reborn, our modern day May Queen, just as Robert is Robin Hood. That's the rebirth signified by the Green Man mentioned by the writer. But who could this other Lady Marion be, I wonder? And what is this reference to jousting?"

"There is another mention of a tower in the poem Little John kept secret too. I wonder to which tower it refers?" said Friar Tuck.

"Have you any idea about the jousting, Thomas? Your family of loyal Time Squires have made weapons for the joust as well as archery," said Sir Richard.

"I was wondering if the tall pole might refer to the May pole of Wellow?" said Thomas.

"Do you joust on the village green?" said Robert.

"Um, not really. It's not big enough," said Thomas. "The knights gather in Nottingham, or Lincoln Castle or occasionally in Edwinstowe. There is a clearing in the forest there."

"Now, wait a minute," said Friar Tuck. "There is a jousting tournament in Lincoln at the moment. That would coincide with the reference to Lincoln in the poem. I have heard many tales from returning squires and knights who have sought your men's protection on their return from this tournament through Sherwood Forest, Sir Richard."

"Actually, there's jousting at Lincoln Castle this weekend in our time as well," said Alice. "I read about it in the newspaper. It sounded really good."

"That sounds like a bit too much of a coincidence," said Friar Tuck. "Perhaps it is like in the poem, *when future meets the past*? I think we should be on our way to fair Lincoln!"

Once again, Robert thought he saw Friar Tuck give a furtive glance around. He wanted to mention it to Alice. There was something about the way the monk could switch from jovial good humour to violent panic that worried Robert. Could it be that Friar Tuck knew more than he was telling them?

"Are we journeying to the Lincoln of my century or yours?" said Sir Richard.

"I don't think it matters to start with," said Alice. "We could always check it out now in your time and then travel to ours if there was nothing interesting."

"The joust is always interesting," said Sir Richard. "I might fancy a try myself. We'd better saddle up the horses and ready the cart, Thomas. And be sure to pack my lance and armour."

"I think we'll opt for the back of the cart if that's O.K?" said Robert. He signalled to Alice not to argue.

"Of course," said Sir Richard. "You are tired."

Alice was about to protest. She was a good rider these days.

"We need to talk," hissed Robert under his breath.

Alice frowned at him but said nothing.

They wandered out to the star lit courtyard where servants were preparing the horses and loading equipment into a cart.

"After you," said Friar Tuck. "I'll ride with you two. I don't think we should let you two out of our sight. We need to protect you."

Robert was annoyed.

"Don't you ride on the back of a horse?" he said to the monk.

"Normally I would," said Friar Tuck. "But this ample frame of mine gets tired these days. I will ride in the cart with you. That way I can guide the horses and we will have no need to endanger any poor servant needlessly."

"That's fine," said Alice. "Actually I am really tired. I think I will sleep anyway."

Robert had to agree. He climbed up after Alice. Friar Tuck nudged the horses into a gentle trot and they set off at a steady pace through the forest trails to Lincoln with Sir Richard and Thomas following behind on horseback. Lulled by the rhythmic rattle of the cart's wheels, Alice fell asleep on Robert's shoulder.

Robert didn't sleep though. There was something worrying him. The words "trust no-one" echoed in his head. He needed to keep awake.

23

Betrayal

The journey was quicker than Robert had imagined despite the rough tracks. They were approaching Lincoln. It was nearly dawn. Robert wondered for a dreadful moment whether he had fallen asleep. He checked his bow and arrows. Alice was still fast asleep.

Friar Tuck was bouncing up and down humming to himself on the driver's seat. Lances, tents and armour rattled in the cart beside them.

The thirteenth century city of Lincoln was tiny compared to the modern one Robert had visited. It was still centred around the remains of the great Roman city called Lindum on the top of the steep hill, a marvellous vantage point from which to see the approach of enemies.

The townsfolk were waking to a new day. Friar Tuck drove the cart over the narrow cobbled streets towards the castle. Robert nudged Alice softly.

"That was the best sleep I've had for ages," yawned Alice. "Oh, you look grumpy. Didn't you sleep?"

Robert grunted.

"Someone's got to stand guard," he said.

"Surely we can relax for a bit. We're among friends," said Alice.

"I'm not so sure," said Robert.

Alice frowned. She closed her eyes. Suddenly she shivered and opened her eyes.

"Actually...you're right," she said. "I can sense evil. Our enemies must be near."

Friar Tuck brought the truck to a standstill. They were in the square, outside the gates of Lincoln Castle. It was much larger than the Castle Square of modern times with fewer buildings that were yet to be built in the coming centuries. The magnificent towers of the cathedral, so familiar to residents and visitors of the modern Lincoln, were not yet built, although most of the rest of the cathedral that Robert had visited was already there, with its enormous medieval stained glass windows like the ancient Dean's Eye. This older, original stone-masonry was breathtakingly beautiful though. Robert noticed that the exquisite sculptures of saints standing proud on their plinths were something he had never seen before and he remembered being told that they had once been hacked out by the vanity of a king who wanted the people to worship only him. Robert couldn't remember which king. He wasn't as good at history as Alice.

"Who is the king nowadays?" he asked Friar Tuck.

"Longshanks," said the monk. "Edward the first would be his proper title."

"Who came after him?" said Robert.

"I would not know since you are talking about my future," said Friar Tuck. "But before him was Henry the third, who came after King John, who, as everyone seems to know, wrote the Magna Carta. A jolly good piece of work that. It's kept here in Lincoln Castle as a matter of fact."

Robert tried to remember all this. It might prove useful in his school lessons. He'd heard of King John. In fact he and Alice had encountered him as a boy with his unpleasant brother Richard in an earlier quest. Robert smiled to himself. They'd been such novices then.

He looked around them. There were colourful tents, some plain and some striped, dotted here and there and horses and people everywhere. Blacksmiths busied themselves repairing hooves, weapons and armour. The fumes from their fires blended with the smell of animals of various kinds, and chickens and cooking meat and bread.

It was very noisy.

"They make ready for this morning's joust," said Friar Tuck. His jolly face creased into an excited smile. "There will be many culinary delicacies to try from far and wide."

He rubbed his belly. Thomas started unloading their equipment.

"I will register your presence, shall I, Sir Richard?" said Friar Tuck. "I shall act as your herald. Perhaps our arrival might encourage a response from certain parties...?"

"I'm not sure that's necessarily a good thing," said Alice. "We came here to see if we can locate the masks. We don't want to invite unwanted trouble."

Friar Tuck glanced furtively around them.

"Let us walk around a bit and see if we can fathom out what the message in the silver box means," said Sir Richard. "We are looking for a tall tower or pole possibly visible from the jousting green."

They wandered between stalls selling snacks of dried game or honeyed fruits. The mead and ale vendors were very busy with long queues. There were also tradesman from afar selling strange artefacts and potions.

"Keep your eyes off the mead, friend," said Sir Richard, playfully patting Friar Tuck.

The fat monk's serious face creased into a smile.

"I think we're right about the poem meaning in Lincoln," said Alice. "This feels right. I feel close to something I must see or do."

"I think I can sense the presence of evil close by too," said Robert.

Alice nodded.

"There are no tall maypoles that I can see," said Thomas scanning the medieval crowd.

"Let's go and watch the jousting," said Friar Tuck. "It's about to start and perhaps it will be helpful?"

They wandered with the gathering crowd through the enormous entrance towers of the castle and under the raised portcullis. They were swept towards the spectator area on one side of the jousting track.

A herald blew on a horn. Everybody looked towards him.

"Ah!" said Sir Richard quietly. "We may have a problem. Look who I see sitting as a guest of honour on the platform."

Robert groaned.

"The Sheriff of Nottingham," he breathed. "He shows up just when you don't want to see him."

"And look who's climbing the platform steps," said Thomas.

"The Prioress of Kirklees," said Alice, frowning.

The Prioress started to look around the crowd. Robert and Alice kept their heads low but she still seemed to be staring in their direction. She was rubbing her neck.

The Sheriff waved his hand to someone in the distance and they heard the grinding sound of the gates being closed.

"I feel bad about this," said Alice.

"How did they know we would be here?" murmured Sir Richard.

"Where is Friar Tuck?" asked Robert.

"Over there..." said Thomas, pointing at the platform. "He's been captured!"

Friar Tuck climbed the steps, held by the Sheriff's men on both sides.

The herald blew his horn again.

"Hear this, good people of Lincoln and special guests!" he announced.

The Sheriff stood up.

"This traitor has been discovered," he shouted to the crowd. "Does anybody speak for him or shall we finally hang him at last?"

"Oh, not again!" said Sir Richard. "Our fat friend needs to take more care. We will have to rescue him again."

"Perhaps I was wrong about him," muttered Robert.

Thomas passed Robert a broad sword and gave Alice his long bow.

"You are a better shot," he said to Alice and bowed courteously.

"You two follow Thomas," said Sir Richard, signalling Robert and Alice. "Cut the friar free when I distract the Sheriff's men."

They pushed their way through the crowd to just below the platform.

"I speak for the monk!" shouted Sir Richard.

He leapt up onto the front of the platform just in front of the important guests. The crowd gasped.

The Sheriff of Nottingham gave a deep, unpleasant laugh.

"Robin Hood? Or are you superseded by a younger model these days, Foliot?" he said. "I hear your days are nearly up."

"Pick up your sword and fight like a man!" said Sir Richard.

The Sheriff drew his weapon. Thomas, Robert and

Alice edged closer to Friar Tuck. Sir Richard lifted his great sword.

He brought it down against the Sheriff's blade and trapped it against the platform floor. The Sheriff laughed and dropped his sword. He lunged towards the Sheriff with a dagger he had hidden in his other hand. It struck Sir Richard in the eye and he fell to the floor moaning.

Robert gripped Alice's arm.

"We have to save Friar Tuck," said Thomas bravely.

Robert could see he was fighting to stay strong.

"Maybe not," said Alice. "I think we should run or time travel."

Robert and Thomas followed Alice's gaze.

Friar Tuck was pointing at them in the crowd.

"There they are!" shouted the monk.

"Seize them!" shouted the Sheriff.

Friar Tuck was no longer a captive. He was standing free at the front of the platform next to the Prioress. Robert felt a sharp point in his back. Men seized him from behind and grabbed his sword. Alice and Thomas were prisoners too.

"The monk betrayed us," said Thomas. His face went scarlet with rage. "I bet the first time he was apparently captured was a trick to trap Alice and Robert too. Tuck, you have betrayed the legend of Robin Hood!" he shouted.

"I knew it!" said Robert. "I tried to talk to you about him, Alice."

The Prioress glided across the platform and smiled cruelly down at them.

"I'll have the box, if you please?" she said holding out her arm.

Robert glanced at Alice. She nodded back. He reached into his blazer and prised the box from where he had jammed it into his pocket, ripping the blazer lining as he pulled it free. The Prioress grabbed it greedily.

"Take them away! I wish to interrogate them shortly," she said. She turned away, cradling the box. "But put the injured knight in my caravan. I will dress Sir Richard's wounds."

The Sheriff's men dragged them towards the castle dungeons.

"Don't let the Prioress touch you, Sir Richard!" shouted Thomas. "She will poison you!"

24

A Desperate Man

It was cold and dark inside this castle. There was a damp, rotten smell in the stale air and Robert heard the squeal of rats and the clank of chains. The moans of prisoners held in the dungeons below filtered up the stone stairway. The guards threw Robert, Alice and Thomas into a small cubicle and slammed the heavy, studded door, bolting it from the outside.

Robert stood with his back against the moist bricks until his eyes adjusted to the darkness. The only light came through a high slit window. Precious sunbeams fanned out like a holy miracle above them.

"Is everybody O.K?" said Robert.

"I'm fine," said Thomas. "I'm just so angry that I trusted Friar Tuck! He has wormed his way into our confidences but all along he was working for the Prioress. I will not forgive his treachery!"

"He must have been a Time Regent won over by the evil side. The Sheriff and the Prioress lured him by his greed no doubt," said Robert.

"We have to get out of here before we settle any scores," said Alice. "Have you still got the jewel, Rob?"

"Yep," said Robert, feeling inside his tatty blazer. "Thank goodness they forgot about the seventh jewel. Let's get out of here. It stinks! Grab my hand Thomas."

"When shall we time travel to?" said Alice.

"Only just into the future and maybe back out in

the courtyard?" said Thomas. "I would like to save my master."

"To think I thought the master you once referred to was the Sheriff of Nottingham, when we first met," said Robert.

"He might be the Friar's master but he is my sworn enemy," said Thomas angrily.

"Let's go, then," said Alice.

They held hands.

"This is the first time I have ever time travelled," said Thomas.

"We are honoured," said Robert grinning. "You'll be fine with us. We will take you into the future. That can be dangerous if you do it for your own selfish reasons but it'll be safe as we're doing it for a quest. You'll miss a few minutes of your life but I guess you'll get them back at the end. Hold tight!"

"It is I who am honoured to be working alongside the heroes of legend," said Thomas.

Robert shrugged. He felt proud, but a chill of fear brushed through him. He tried to push it away and look brave. He closed his eyes and they began to travel. Robert concentrated his thoughts and aligned them with Alice. He focused his energy on where and when they wanted to go.

It was very quick. The tunnel flashed in and out of existence and propelled them through the mighty castle walls and just a little into Thomas's future. Very soon they were back out in the sunshine and among the throng of spectators, squires and knights.

The joust had started. Everyone was watching eagerly as two armoured knights with full helmets and visors lifted their lances and prepared to charge.

"Wow! How cool is that!" said Robert.

The enormous horses galloped forward sending dust clouds billowing into the audience. Everyone held their breath, including Robert. The riders clashed. The lance of one struck the other in the centre of the chest catapulting him, almost in slow motion, from his saddle, like a floppy puppet.

"Ouch! That looks nasty," said Robert.

"Come, friends," said Thomas. "The Sheriff and the Prioress are no longer on the platform."

Robert noticed that the castle gate was open again.

"It's her!" hissed Thomas. "The Prioress is leaving. It is her caravan and escort. We must follow."

"Just a minute," said Alice. "What about the masks?"

"That is for you to decide, my Lady," said Thomas. "Perhaps you need to stay here. But I must follow my master."

"Alone?" said Alice.

"Do not fear for me," said Thomas. "I will follow until I know where she is taking him. Then I will alert the archers and swordsmen of Sherwood Forest and we will attack. I will also dispatch a party to deal with the traitor monk."

"Good luck," said Robert. "I think Alice is right. Our duty lies here."

Thomas bowed and disappeared off into the crowd.

"So what's the plan?" said Robert.

He turned around to Alice.

"Oh, no!" he gasped. "Alice...!"

The Sheriff of Nottingham held Alice around the shoulders with one arm. In his other hand was his dagger. The point scratched her neck and sent a trickle of blood down onto the collar of her dirty white blouse.

"Stay very still," said the Sheriff. "Keep your

hands where I can see them clearly."

"But you have the box," said Robert.

"She has the box..." hissed the Sheriff, nodding towards the cloud of dirt leaving a track behind the retreating horses of the Prioress of Kirklees.

"Has she left you?" said Robert.

"Don't try and be smart," said the Sheriff. He tightened his grip on Alice, squeezing the air from her lungs. She was struggling to breathe. "Now tell me where the masks are?"

"We don't know," said Robert. "That's the truth."

"I don't believe you!" roared the Sheriff. "Tell me! If you do not, I will kill your Lady Marion."

Robert was beginning to feel very scared now. He hoped it did not show. For a moment he did not know what he should do. Alice was starting to lose consciousness. Her face was pale and blue.

Then he had an idea. It would be very tricky, but if he could hold onto Alice as he pretended to hand over the Time Trigger perhaps he could somehow get them back to their own time.

"You are a sick, desperate man," he said, taking a step forwards and stretching out his hand.

Then he lunged and let a surge of will power fly through his soul, directing his thoughts forward in time. He clung on tight to Alice's hand.

Inside the Time Tunnel he felt a sharp, cold pain. Something had cut into his arm. Deeper into the spiral of time they fell. Robert tried to open his eyes but the whiteness of the tunnel's energy was too bright. He started to be sick. Fear and pain and white hot evil tore into his body. He screamed out in agony.

Another voice called then. A lady's voice. It was calm and soft. "Reach out for me!" said the voice.

Robert forced his arm out and the tunnel col-

130

lapsed. He fell very hard onto cool ground. He opened his eyes. The bright sunlight was dim compared to the extreme conditions in the tunnel. He stood up. Blood trickled down from the skin wound on his arm.

Alice was lying on the floor, panting. He took a step towards her but she held her hand up, signalling that she was alright. He drew in his breath and span around to meet the darkness that he felt behind them.

25

Lady M

To Robert's surprise the Sheriff was kneeling on all fours on the modern grassy courtyard of Lincoln Castle. A woman dressed in a Lincoln green skirt and jacket held a broadsword to his neck. Dark hair was neatly bound into hairnet cauls on either side of her face beneath her short veil and coronet.

It was evening. The castle was closed. But all around them were the empty stalls and tents laid out for the mock joust tomorrow.

"I hoped that one day we would meet," said the woman.

"Who are you?" said Alice, slowly standing up next to Robert.

"My name is Lady Margaret Foliot," she said.

"The Lady M who wrote the poem in the box?" said Robert.

She smiled.

"I am one of us," she said smiling. "You are my namesake reborn, Alice. But yes. I wrote the poetry. I am Sir Richard's great grand daughter. In my time I am the guardian of the masks. I also lead the men and women of Sherwood from my home at Wellow Castle. We serve our God and are loyal to the King. As for selfish schemers like some, who pretend to lead, like this one...."

The Sheriff tried to speak. Lady Margaret pushed the sword deeper against his shoulder.

"Keep still, traitor!" she said, shaking her head. "Politicians! I have yet to speak with one I could trust."

"What did you do just now...in the tunnel?" said Robert.

"Intercepted it to combat the evil intentions of this power crazed idiot," she jabbed the Sheriff again. "I was sleeping and I felt a shadow of evil cross my soul so I used the Shell of Destiny. I saw what was about to happen and I time travelled towards your energy. We will meet just this one time. I can only travel forwards this once. My destiny lies in my own time to protect my people. That is the path I have chosen. I will take this idiot back with me to my world and my people will decide what must be done to punish him for his crimes. The chivalric code dictates that justice must be done."

"But can you tell us where to find the masks?" said Alice.

"I do not need to," said Lady Margaret. "You will see. And I must not risk betrayal to his ears or any others. It is your destiny. You have the sight and the knowledge to do what is right. You are the guardians now. I did my duty when I travelled back and moved the masks from the forest where I knew the clever Prioress might find them. I told no-one. Not even Little John had worked it out. As her powers grew, the Prioress would have been able to time travel even without the jewel or any Time Trigger. She would have found a way to go back and find out where the masks were buried and I couldn't risk that. It would alter your destinies and expose the masks."

Lady Margaret Foliot put her hand on the Sheriff's shoulders.

"I must go now before this one escapes," she said.

"Thank you," said Alice.

"And I thank you for what you will yet do. For good to triumph you must fulfil your destinies and become mighty Time Regents."

She closed her eyes. Robert and Alice stepped back from the flare of the Tunnel she had willed into being. Lady Margaret and the Sheriff of Nottingham vanished. The Time Tunnel was there and gone in an instant, almost invisible to anybody unaware of time travel lore, leaving the characteristic circle of scorch marks smoking in the grass.

Robert heard the angry Sheriff's cry as he was swept back by Lady Margaret to face his doom. It turned to a scream of fear as the medieval sounds faded into silence.

Robert looked at Alice. She fell into his arms in a hug of relief. They stood there quietly, feeling the pounding of each other's hearts and the gentle rush of air with every breath.

"That was too close," said Alice. "He nearly squashed me to death. I'd rather die shooting my arrows or something."

Robert laughed.

"Born hero, are you?" he said.

He was about to suggest they go and get a tasty snack from the amazing ice-cream parlour that stayed open late on Steep Hill when he saw the change in Alice's expression. She was looking up, over the castle walls, towards the modern day profile of the towers of Lincoln Cathedral.

"That's it!" she shouted. "Look! In between the castle flagpoles. I do have the sight. I'm *looking on high*, like the poem says, and I can see *Lincoln's Tower*. Like the poem, it is *the view from the jousting green*. I can see the big central tower. It wasn't built yet in the last years of the thirteenth century when we were just there. We couldn't have seen it then. I bet it was built in Lady Margaret's time in the fourteenth century and it's certainly there now. We just had to come to our time to this jousting green to see it."

"So, your shadow is in fact Lady Margaret. We are the descendents," said Robert, working it all out. "We all stood here as was our destiny and she said you would see it. Maid Marion-Alice, the May Queen, I think you're right! I think the masks may be hidden up there."

"Come on!" called Alice, running towards the exit.

They jumped over the barriers and ran across the Castle Square. There were not many people about now. It was a warm evening and a few adults sat outside the *Magna Carta* pub with drinks. Someone walked by with a Dalmatian puppy and a runner jogged in the opposite direction.

Alice ran around the cathedral looking up. Robert followed her, skirting the vast fourteenth century front towers that rose up and almost touched the clouds. Alice carried on along the cobbles around the south side, in front of the Bishop's Palace. Robert noticed the empty plinths where he knew great sculptures of the saints and apostles had once stood. He had seen them with his own eyes.

"Bet it was Henry the Eighth who had them chopped off," he thought to himself.

"It's hopeless!" said Alice after a few minutes. She stood, panting, on the grass beside the Galilee Porch. "It's too vast and too high. We could never get up there even if we knew where to look."

They heard the cry of a bird of prey above them and craned their necks. A flurry of white feathers began to drift from the masonry far above.

"It's the peregrine falcon that nests high up on the big tower," said Robert. "I heard about it on the news on television. I think it's just eaten a smaller bird for dinner."

They followed the white feathers as they gently drifted in the air currents, down and down to the grass below.

"There are loads of feathers all around here, like bones after a giant has eaten anything that climbs up its bean stalk," said Alice, examining the grass at the foot of the great central tower. "It's a bit gruesome."

The falcon cried again and they looked up.

"Hey, wait a minute..." said Alice. "Look up there near the falcon's ledge. There are two face things, like miniature gargoyles. Actually, they look like two of those green men. They've got leaves coming out of their ears."

"I can't really see from here," said Robert. "We need to get hold of a pair of binoculars. Just a minute..." He fumbled in his pocket. "Here we are. These belonged to Mr Reynolds."

They looked at each other for a second. Alice's freckled face went pale.

"Poor Mr Reynolds," she said.

Robert aimed the binoculars at the two masks. Their weathered surfaces looked just like the stonework all around. No-one would ever know these bearded effigies were not ordinary green men carvings.

"Brilliant hiding place," said Robert.

"Oh...!"

Alice stumbled. She clutched her head and sank down to her knees.

"What is it, Alice?" said Robert, kneeling down beside her.

"Don't you feel it? The power surge when you look at them. It was awesome," said Alice. "That's them, I'm sure. At last. We've found the Masks of Robin Hood."

26

The Masks of Robin Hood

Robert squinted through the binoculars towards where more white feathers floated out from the falcon's haunt so very high above them. Then he felt it too. His body shook with a pulse of energy as his eyes connected with the secret Time Triggers. They were difficult to see in detail but Robert could make out the eyes and three little bumps across the foreheads.

"They are green men," said Robert. "Much smaller than I imagined masks to be. Do you think those bumps above the eyes have got the six precious stones underneath?"

"Yes," said Alice. "The masks are weathered with age nowadays and beautifully camouflaged. I bet Lady Margaret had help to hide them way up there when the tower was actually being built," said Alice.

Robert felt quite dizzy. He had to stop looking at them. He was starting to feel sick again.

"How do we get them down?" he said.

Alice was thinking.

"I'm not sure we do," she said after a minute or two.

"What do you mean?" said Robert. "We can't have been sent on this quest to find these things and then leave them."

"But we were brought on this journey by the evil Prioress and the Sheriff. They wanted us to help them to take them. But our true destiny is to be the guardians. Perhaps it is just our job to let them stay where they are safe and tell no-one."

Robert screwed his face up.

"I'm not sure," he said.

"That would actually be an awesome responsibility," said Alice.

"It would make us the target of evil time travellers for ever," said Robert.

"Yes," said Alice. "It would."

Robert sighed deeply.

"We'd never be able to relax," he said. "We'd be on duty permanently. We could still be killed."

"Like Little John," said Alice. "He never grew old. He stayed as a Regent for years and years."

"Let's give this some thought," said Robert. He slumped against the cathedral wall. "How are we going to get home anyway?"

"I don't think I'm going home," said Alice.

She sat down next to Robert.

"You mean you're going to sleep out here under the stars?" he said.

"No. I mean ever," said Alice.

"Hang on," said Robert. "I never thought time travelling would be like this. I don't want to be some superhero Time Regent if that means I have to roam around the galaxies for the good of the universe for ever. I want to be normal too."

He looked at Alice. A tear trickled down her cheek.

"But we're not normal, are we?" she said. "We have to stop pretending, Rob."

"I think we could choose not to be different," said Robert. He took her hand. "We could decide we don't want to use our powers again."

"Then who would be the guardians of the masks?" said Alice.

Robert shook his head. If they decided to walk

away from all this, would the Prioress find the masks somehow? Maybe others would come. Because they were time travellers, Alice and Robert could feel the power of the masks drawing into their souls just by looking at them. If they fell into the hands of a time traveller who had evil plans to start wars or wipe out whole countries, he knew the masks' powers would be the key to their victory. To be able to time travel anywhere and anytime, to alter destinies and find out secrets and steal anything... the masks would be the most valuable tools. And what if such people found out that he and Alice knew where they were? They might torture them. The more he thought about it, the more depressed he felt.

"The Prioress!" he said suddenly. "She's got Sir Richard. What if Thomas needs us?"

"Do you think we ought to travel back and find out?" asked Alice.

Robert nodded.

"I think there's unfinished business there," he said. "We know the masks are safe for now."

Alice stood up and brushed the grass from her skirt.

"Some clean clothes would be nice. And a shower," she said. "I don't think we can ever go back and show our uniform to the teachers or our parents!"

Robert grinned at her. Alice's smile made him feel more confident. He took her hands in his.

"Where to?" he said.

"Let our powers direct us," said Alice. "Concentrate on Sir Richard Foliot and we should end up wherever he is."

Once again they travelled through time, engulfed in corridors of matter across the caverns of space. The journey was a little bumpy. As they landed,

Robert remembered he had not been holding the jewel Time Trigger. Just Alice. They didn't need to actually hold a Trigger then. Their inner strength was enough.

They were in a gloomy hallway. A statue of the Virgin Mary smiled down on them. A pitcher of water and a wash bowl stood ready to be used on a simple wooden table.

"Where are we?" said Alice.

"In the gatehouse of my priory at Kirklees in Yorkshire," said a woman's voice behind them.

They span round to see again the gaunt, malicious face of the Prioress.

"What have you done with Sir Richard?" said Robert.

"In the chamber within," said the Prioress, pointing towards the arched door beside the pitcher and bowl. "He is mortally wounded. My bleeding techniques are common medical practice in this age but as an experienced time traveller, I know of course that this will hasten his death. And now that you two have walked straight into my house, I will have your lives as well and vanquish forever the legend of Robin Hood."

27

The Last Arrow

The Prioress drew a dagger from her robes.

"The tip of this is poisoned," she said. "One scratch and you will die an agonising death."

She cackled and took a step towards Robert.

"You do not have the masks," said Alice.

"I have John's charts. I am beginning to make sense of some of the poetry. I will find them eventually, with or without you," said the Prioress. "Of course you could just tell me all that you know and I will spare your lives?"

"Ha! You'd never keep your word!" said Robert.

"As you wish..." said the Prioress.

She advanced closer to them.

Somebody shouted from outside.

In that instant Robert seized his chance. He grabbed the pitcher and flung it at the Prioress, catching her by surprise and sending her slight frame tumbling to the floor covered in water. The poisoned dagger span across the wooden floorboards.

Robert grabbed the bowl and smashed it down over her head. She fell back, dazed, surrounded by broken pottery.

Alice picked up the dagger and pointed it towards the snarling Prioress.

At the same time, footsteps leapt up the stairs. An archer wearing Lincoln Green and brandishing a sword bounded towards them.

"Thomas!" shouted Robert.

"My friends!" said Thomas. "How pleased I am to

find you here. I see that really you did not need my aid or my weapons. You have defeated our foe with water and clay!"

Robert and Thomas shook hands.

"The men of Robin Hood found our fat monk and like the ballads say, they killed a traitorous clergyman. I will spare you the details. Now where is Sir Richard?" said Thomas.

Robert nodded towards the door.

"No! You shall not win!" screamed the Prioress.

She launched herself at Robert, brushing past the poisoned dagger in Alice's hand.

"Finish it!" said Thomas, tossing Robert his sword.

Robert held the sword with both his sweaty hands, its tip outstretched towards the Prioress.

"Stay back!" he shouted at her.

His heart raced. To Robert's surprise, the Prioress stopped. But she was not looking at Robert and his sword.

"Oh, no!" whispered Alice.

She dropped the dagger. There was a tiny blood stain on the blade.

Robert knew the poison must have entered the Prioress' blood.

The Prioress clutched the wound on her arm.

"What have you done?" she screamed at Alice.

She ran to the stairs. Robert started to follow but Thomas caught his arm.

"Leave her, friend," said Thomas. "Sir Richard's men have the gatehouse and the priory surrounded. She will not get far."

They heard her screaming outside.

"She will die," said Alice. "The dagger was poisoned. Is there nothing we can do?"

Thomas shook his head. He opened the door to the

chamber. Sir Richard lay on a wooden bed propped up on pillows. He smiled weakly at them.

"Are the masks safe?" he said.

"Yes," said Robert and Alice together.

"Then do not mourn for me, my friends," said Sir Richard. "My time is done. My sons and daughters will carry on the Foliot name and the care of our people and our way of life. Thomas, my faithful Squire, will give them everything they need."

Thomas bowed low and nodded.

"Sir Richard, can I ask you something?" said Robert.

The wounded knight held out his hand and drew Robert closer.

"Is it about being a guardian?" he said.

"How did you know?" said Robert.

"I can see the burden weighs heavy. It shows in your face," said Sir Richard. "You know exactly how to reach Thomas and the Shell of Destiny in the castle cavern if you need it. But I think you will find your own ways. High Regents do. Each one is quite unique. Trust each other and your own instincts and you will find a way."

"Alice is so strong, but I'm not sure that I...well...that I'm brave enough," said Robert.

"That you have the courage to question is all the strength you need," said Sir Richard. "You will both be fine. You have many great quests ahead of you. This is only one. Robin Hood is just one of your names."

He flopped back into Thomas' arms.

"Let me fire one last arrow through the window," said Sir Richard. "You can bury me where it lands."

Thomas and Robert propped Sir Richard up and Alice helped him clip his arrow into place. She gently turned his body sideways and helped him to pull the flaxen bowstring back across his chest.

He loosed the arrow. It flew gracefully across the turquoise sky.

Robert looked across at Alice. She was strong and beautiful and clever. But most of all she was smiling back at him. Their destinies were intertwined. Power and knowledge soared through him like an arrow and in that moment he knew that he had made his choice. The eternal pathways of time would be their stormy playground. He knew there could be no other way.